Sophie's
Further Adventures

First published individually as *Sophie in the Saddle* (1993),
Sophie Is Seven (1994) and *Sophie's Lucky* (1995) by Walker Books Ltd
87 Vauxhall Walk, London SE11 5HJ

This edition published 2006

8 10 9

Text © 1993, 1994, 1995 Fox Busters Ltd
Illustrations © 1991, 1993, 1994, 1995 David Parkins
Cover illustrations © 1991, 1993, 1994, 1999 David Parkins

The right of Dick King-Smith and David Parkins to be identified as
author and illustrator respectively of this work has been asserted by them
in accordance with the Copyright, Designs and Patents Act 1988

This book has been typeset in Giovanni

Printed and bound in Great Britain by Clays Ltd, St Ives plc

British Library Cataloguing in Publication Data:
a catalogue record for this book is available from the British Library

ISBN 978-1-84428-992-9

www.walker.co.uk

Sophie's
Further Adventures

Dick King-Smith

illustrated by
David Parkins

WALKER BOOKS
AND SUBSIDIARIES

LONDON • BOSTON • SYDNEY • AUCKLAND

Contents

Sophie
in the
Saddle

Contents

Puddle

Sophie's birthday was on the twenty-fifth of December. Sophie was rather proud of this fact. Ages and ages ago, when she was only four, Sophie had said to her twin brothers Matthew and Mark, "I bet I'm the only girl who was ever born on Christmas Day."

"Course you're not," they said.

"Well, who else was then?" Sophie said. "Go on, tell me."

The twins looked at one another.

"I know!" said Matthew.

"I know what you're going to say!" said Mark.

"Jesus!" they cried.

Sophie looked scornful.

"Funny sort of girl," she said.

She plodded off to ask her mother and father, but they said that thousands of babies were born every day of the year, including Christmas Day.

"So there must be lots of other little girls who share your birthday," her mother said.

"I bet I'm the only one who's going to be a lady farmer," said Sophie.

"Well, that narrows it down a bit," said her father, "but I expect there are quite a number who share your ambition."

"What's an ambition?"

"Something you are determined to do."

Sophie, though small, was very determined, and she was not going to lose this argument.

"I bet," she said, "that I'm the only girl in the world who was born on Christmas Day and is going to be a lady farmer and is going to have a cow called Blossom and two hens called April and May and a pony called Shorty and a pig called Measles."

"Now there," they said, "you may be right."

All that was two years before. Sophie was six now, and the twins were eight – Matthew, as he always would be, ten minutes older than Mark.

Sophie was as determined as ever to be a lady farmer one day. For two years she had been saving up for this. On the side of her

piggy-bank was stuck a notice.

Originally it had said:

But since going to school, Sophie's spelling had improved, and now it read:

Farm monney
thank you
Sophie

At one time there had been ten pounds and twenty pence in the piggy-bank, but Sophie had spent three pounds of this on a collar and lead for one of her pets. These were a black cat called Tomboy, a white rabbit called Beano and a puppy, as yet without a name. Strictly speaking, the puppy belonged to all the family, but already

Sophie thought of it as her own.

It had arrived this very day, her sixth birthday, the seventh Christmas Day of her life.

In fact Sophie had last used the collar and lead for Beano, so that he could exercise on the lawn, the loop of the lead dropped over a stake round which he grazed in a circle.

"The puppy can have the rabbit's collar and lead now, can't he?" Sophie's mother said that evening.

"No," said Sophie.

"Beano doesn't need them," said Sophie's father. "He's in his nice warm hutch for the winter. And in the summer you can always tether him with a bit of string."

"No," said Sophie.

"Why not?" they said.

"Because I bought them with my farm money.

They're mine. And you said the puppy belongs to all of us. So I'll sell you all the collar and lead. You can all pay me for them."

"Not me," said Mark.

"Nor me," said Matthew.

"How much?" said Sophie's father.

Sophie rubbed the tip of her nose, a sure sign that she was thinking deeply.

"To you lot – three pounds, fifty pence," she said.

"How much did you pay for them in the first place?" her mother asked. Sophie did not approve of telling lies.

"Three pounds," she said.

"You're asking more than when they were new!"

"Take it or leave it," said Sophie.

Her father took his pipe out of his mouth to give an admiring whistle.

"Quite the business woman," he said. "I can just see you at market. You'll drive a hard bargain."

"I shan't," said Sophie. "I shall drive a Land Rover."

She sat on the floor beside the Christmas tree, the new puppy in her lap. He was a little terrier, white except for a black patch over his right eye.

"You haven't got a name, my dear," she said.

"We could call him Pirate," her father said.

"Why?"

"Because he's got a black patch over one eye."

"Or just Patch?" said Sophie's mother.

"Call him Mark," said Matthew.

"Or Matthew," said Mark, and they both giggled.

"You know what you are," said Sophie.

"Yes," they said, for they knew only too well what an angry Sophie always called them. "We're

mowldy, stupid and assive!" they chanted,
and they rolled about, laughing.

"You're ingerant, you are," said
Sophie.

"Ignorant, you mean," they said.

"That too," Sophie said.

She put the puppy down and plodded off, shoulders hunched, the picture of disapproval.

"Come on now, Sophie," said her mother. "You choose a name."

"After all, it was you who liked this puppy best," her father said. "Andrew's dad told me."

Sophie's friend Andrew was a farmer's son, and their terrier Lucy was the mother of the nameless puppy.

Sophie turned round.

"Can we call him whatever I choose?" she said.

"If you like."

"Promise?"

"Oh, all right."

At that moment the puppy plodded off into a corner of the room. Here it squatted down and did a little pool on the carpet.

"Look at that!" cried the twins.

Sophie rubbed the tip of her nose.

"That's it," she said.

"What's what?" said her parents.

"What he's done. It's given me an idea for a name."

"What?" said everybody.

"Puddle," said Sophie. "Let's call him Puddle."

"Sophie!" said her mother.

"Ugh!" said her brothers.

"Give a dog a bad name," said her father.

"You promised," said Sophie.

So Puddle he was.

Jolly Brave

Apart from that first mistake, Puddle did not live up to his name. By the time Sophie and the boys went back to school after the Christmas holidays, he was pretty well house-trained.

This was largely due to Sophie's efforts. She watched Puddle like a hawk, and the moment he seemed restless or showed any sign of being about to lower himself towards the floor, she scooped him up and put him out in the garden.

All this in turn was thanks to Sophie's Aunt Al.

Aunt Al was really the children's great-great-aunt but she was also Sophie's great great friend. She was nearly eighty-two years old but extremely young at heart, and she lived in the Highlands, a mysterious-sounding land, Sophie always thought, from which the inhabitants peered down at the rest of the world far below.

It was Aunt Al who had fixed it so that Sophie was allowed to keep a stray black cat, at first called Tom, but later, after giving birth to four kittens, renamed Tomboy.

It was Aunt Al who now owned one of those kittens, called Ollie.

It was Aunt Al who had given Sophie the rabbit, Beano.

And it was Aunt Al who telephoned, a couple of days after Christmas.

Sophie answered the phone.

"It's Aunt Al," she said. "She's ringing down from the Highlands."

"Ringing up, you mean," said her father.

Sophie sighed.

"Oh, Daddy," she said. Sophie, in common with her great-great-aunt, liked to speak her mind, but she was wary of telling her father that he was mowldy, stupid and assive. But really! How could you ring *up* from the top of the Highlands?

"She wants to speak to you, I expect," said Sophie.

"Who's 'she'? The cat's mother?" said a sharp voice at the other end. "It's you I want to speak to, Sophie."

"Oh."

"You got a nice surprise, didn't you?"

"Oh, yes. Puddle, you mean."

25

"Is that what the puppy's called?"

"Yes," said Sophie.

"That's what I'm ringing you about," said Aunt Al. "I know he's meant to be the family's pet, but your father has his work, and your mother has the house to look after, and the boys won't be the slightest use – always off playing football – so you're going to have to be the dog-trainer, Sophie. He's too young to be taught a lot of things yet, but you must get him house-trained. I'll tell you what to do." And she did.

"And if he slips up," said Aunt Al, "don't let anyone shout at him or rub his nose in it – he won't understand. Oh, and by the way, soda water's good for the carpet."

The conversation ended in their usual no-nonsense way.

"Got it?"

"Yes."

"OK. Ollie sends his love."

"Right."

"Bye."

"Bye."

Sophie put the phone down.

"What was all that about?" asked her mother.

Sophie did not answer directly. Instead she said, "Mum. When was I clean?"

"Clean? Potty-trained, you mean?"

"Yes."

"Oh, about two."

"Two months?"

"Two years!"

"Yikes!" said Sophie.

She picked up the puppy and went out into the

garden and put him down on the lawn.

"Now then, my dear," she said, "you haven't even got two weeks before I go back to school, so you'd better get a move on," and when he did, she said, "You *are* clever."

"*Mia-ow*?" said a voice, and Tomboy came to rub against her legs. Puddle immediately made a bumbling rush at the cat and received a sharp cuff round the ear.

"*Nee-o!*" said Tomboy – or that's what it sounded like – and stalked off.

"Come and see Beano," Sophie said. "He won't hurt you."

Beano lived in a large hutch in the potting-shed, where once, when younger, Sophie had kept her flocks and herds of woodlice, worms, centipedes, earwigs, slugs and snails.

He was a large white rabbit with floppy ears and pink eyes and a wiffly nose. He had never been in the least afraid of Tomboy, and now, when Sophie opened the hutch door and put him down on the floor beside the puppy, he thumped with his hind legs and gave such a threatening growl that Puddle's small tail went between his legs. "Nobody loves you, my dear," Sophie said, "except your trainer."

*   *   *

By the end of the school holidays Puddle had learned a lot.

Not to do things – or chew things – in the house.

Not to tangle with cats or rabbits.

To answer to his name.

To walk – after a fashion – on a lead beside Sophie, wearing Beano's old blue collar.

Sophie got up early on the first day of the new term, and dressed – grey pleated skirt, grey shirt, striped tie, maroon cardigan. At first she had hated her school uniform, but now she was used to it, and by the time she had attended to all her animals no one would have guessed that her clothes had been clean a mere half-hour before. Her dark hair looked, as always, as though she had just come through a hedge backwards.

"Looking forward to school, Sophie?" her father said at breakfast.

"Sort of," Sophie said.

She quite liked school and was interested in some of the things they taught her. It was just a pity there were no Farming Lessons, nor did they allow you to bring pets.

"You will look after Puddle properly, Mum, won't you?" she said.

"Of course I will."

"He's still only amateur, you see."

"Amateur?"

"Yes, you know, young."

"Oh, you mean immature," her mother said.

"An infant," said Matthew.

"Like Sophie," said Mark, for Sophie, of course, was still in the infants, while the twins were juniors.

"And all her little friends," said Matthew.

"Like Duncan," said Mark.

Duncan was a small, fat boy whom Sophie had once considered employing as a farm worker at some time in the future.

"He's a wally," said Sophie.

"And Dawn," said Matthew.

"Yuk!" said Sophie.

Dawn was a pretty little girl with golden hair done in bunches. Sophie had often been tempted to give her a bunch of fives. They did not get on.

"And Andrew," said Mark.

"Sophie fancies Andrew," they giggled.

Sophie's face darkened, but before she could utter her usual comment her father said, "Wonder if they've sold the other five pups?"

Sophie forgot about her brothers' teasing and looked thoughtful.

"Suppose there was just one left," she said. "All alone."

"No, Sophie," said her father firmly. "We are not having any more animals in this house."

That evening Sophie lay in the bath, playing with a very lifelike rubber frog.

Puddle sat on the bath mat, whining. Perhaps on account of his name he seemed to love water. He liked to jump in any pools left lying after the rain, and he longed to join Sophie in the bath. School had been much as Sophie had expected. Dawn was just as yucky, Duncan was just as much of a wally, Andrew was just as nice, and they still didn't give Farming Lessons.

Lucy's other puppies had all been sold, Andrew told her, but he had asked her and Puddle to tea

next Saturday, which was nice.
Or rather Sophie had told Andrew
to ask his mother to ask them,
which she did.

Sophie squeezed the
rubber frog's stomach

and it let out a loud squeak, much to Puddle's
excitement. Her mother came into the bathroom
in time to hear Sophie say, "This is a frog and
he's amphigorous."

"He's amphibious," her mother said.

"That's what I said," replied Sophie, launching
the frog back into the water.

"Wish I could swim," she said.

"Can you swim?" she said to Andrew next
Saturday, as they went on a tour of the farmyard,
Andrew leading, Sophie plodding behind,
Puddle following.

"Yes, course I can," said Andrew, his stock
answer. If Sophie had asked whether he could fly,
the reply would probably have been the same.

"I'm a brilliant swimmer, I am," he said.

"Matthew and Mark can swim like fishes," Sophie said, "but I can't."

Just then they came upon the duck pond. It was a large duck pond, and round its rim a number of ducks were standing and preening their feathers. At the sight of them Puddle ran forward, yapping with excitement, and the ducks, quacking with dismay, took to the water. Puddle leaped in after them.

"He'll be drowned!" shouted Sophie, and she jumped in after Puddle.

Andrew's father, attracted by all the noise, arrived in time to see a remarkable scene.

On the bank Andrew was rolling about, laughing fit to bust.

In the pond the puppy was swimming round and round with an expert doggy paddle in pursuit of the ducks.

Sophie was standing waist deep in the filthy water. "Yuk!" she cried. "I'm stuck in the duck-muck!"

"Andrew's dad pulled me out," Sophie said later, at home.

"You didn't half stink," said Mark.

"You still do," said Matthew.

"The first time you went to that farm," Sophie's mother said, "you fell in a cowpat."

"Why ever did you jump into the duck pond?" her father said.

"I thought Puddle would drown," Sophie said. "I didn't know he could swim."

"But you can't. And it might have been deep."

"I didn't think of that," Sophie said.

Matthew and Mark looked at their small but determined sister. Then they looked at one another.

Then, with one voice, they said, "You were jolly brave."

Sophie grinned.

"Was I?" she said.

"One thing's certain," said her father. "It's high time you learned to swim."

"And before the end of the summer term too," her mother said.

"Why?" said Sophie.

"Because we're all going on holiday to the seaside this year."

"Yikes!" cried Sophie. "All of us?"

"Yes."

"Tomboy?"

"No."

"Beano?"

"No."

Sophie put on her most determined face.

"If Puddle can't go," she said, "I'm not coming."

"If you learn to swim, properly," her father said, "then Puddle can come."

"I'll learn," said Sophie.

A Nasty Shock

Sophie was as good as her word. In the summer term the schoolchildren went, once a week, to the local swimming baths, and by half-term Sophie had swum a width. She was not a graceful swimmer like Matthew and Mark, who could do a flashy crawl. Both twins were fast runners, winning all their races at the school sports, and swimming for them was just another form of racing.

Sophie, by contrast, sploshed along, using a

stroke much like Puddle's, but she kept doggedly
on, blowing like a grampus, determined not to
give up. Just before the end of term, she swam
a length of the baths.

She came out of school with a big grin on
her face.

"You look pleased with yourself," her mother
said. "What have you been up to?"

"I done it!" said Sophie.

"Done what – I mean, did what?"

"Swum a length of the baths. I can swim
properly. So Puddle can come with us to the
seaside, can't he?"

The twins came racing up, dead-heating
as usual.

"Mum!" they shouted in unison. "Sophie's
swum a length!"

"She wasn't very fast," said Matthew. "She took ages."

"But she kept going," said Mark, "and she never put her feet down on the bottom once."

"Course not," said Sophie. She did not approve of cheating.

The whole conversation was repeated that evening, when the children's father returned from work.

"Well done, Sophie," he said and he looked at his wife.

"We can tell them now, can't we?" he said and she nodded.

"Tell us what?" they all said.

"Well, you see, the idea of taking Puddle with us complicated things a bit. Hotels and boarding-houses don't allow dogs. So we're going to stay somewhere

where they do. It's only about three miles from the sea, so we can get to the beach in no time."

"And I think you'll all like it," said the children's mother."

"Especially Sophie."

"Why specially me?" said Sophie.

"Because we're going to stay on a farm."

Sophie's cry of *"Yikes!"* was the loudest they had ever heard. When her parents came to say good night to her that evening, she was lying in bed looking at pictures on her bedroom wall, the four pictures, drawn by her mother, of Blossom, of April and May, of Shorty, and of Measles.

"Will they have spotty pigs on this farm?" she said.

"Don't know. Perhaps. It says they have all sorts of different animals."

"Cows?"

"Probably."

"And hens?"

"Sure to."

"And Shetland ponies?"

"Don't know about Shetlands. They've got ponies. For riding."

"Yikes!" said Sophie very softly. "I could ride."

"You'll have to learn how to, properly," they said.

"I'll learn," said Sophie.

The final days of the summer term dragged by, but at last came the magic moment when the car was loaded and the family, and Puddle, were ready to set off for Cornwall and the sea.

"Don't forget my wellies," Sophie had said when they were packing.

"Wellies? On the beach?"

"On the farm," Sophie said.

Tomboy and Beano were to be looked after by a kind neighbour during the two weeks' holiday. Sophie had given strict instructions about their welfare.

"There's plenty of hay and rabbit-mixture for Beano," she said, "and what sort of bread do you have?"

"Wholemeal," said the neighbour. "Why?"

"He likes that," Sophie said. "The crusts. If you could spare some now and then? Lightly toasted."

Tomboy was to have the run of the kitchen via the cat-flap. "But," said Sophie, "she is to have water to drink, not milk, it makes her fat. But she can have as much tinned cat-food as she wants."

"Won't that make her fat?" said the neighbour.

"No," said Sophie. "It's full of protons and carbonhydrons, all different flavours, her favourite's Rabbit."

Now Sophie sat between the boys on the back seat, Puddle on her lap. He was nine months old now and as well trained as small terriers ever can be, which isn't very well, as a rule.

He would walk on a lead without pulling, and come when called, and sit when told, but the command "Stay!" didn't mean much to him since he liked always to be on the go.

"He'll love the sea, won't he?" said Sophie.

"We all shall, I hope," said her mother. "Especially if this fine weather keeps up. Let's just hope it doesn't rain."

"Farmers need rain," said Sophie.

47

"Not while we're on holiday they don't," said
her father.

"Or only at night," said her mother.

It was a long drive, and it was almost dark by the
time they arrived, too late to think of going to a
beach that day. But the farmer and his wife were
very welcoming and they had a daughter
of about Sophie's age called Jo.

When she was introduced, Sophie
eyed Jo with some suspicion for she
was quite a pretty girl, not unlike
the dreaded Dawn to look at.
However, she wore her fair hair
short, and she had a friendly smile.
More, she was wearing wellies and
old scruffy clothes and she smelt

quite strongly of pig, so Sophie was reassured.

Next morning, Sophie woke up early and looked out of the window of the funny little attic room that was to be hers and Puddle's for the two weeks.

She could see cows coming in for milking, and sheep in a field, and ponies in a paddock, and hens and ducks and geese in the yard, and she knew there must be at least one pig because of the smell of the farmer's daughter.

So she got dressed and tiptoed downstairs, Puddle following, and put on her wellies and went out. Jo, she found, was up already, crossing the yard with a bucket in her hand and a couple of collies at her heels, and she said "Hello," and the farm dogs sniffed at Puddle and wagged their tails.

"Hello," Sophie said. "Have you got pigs?"

"One," said Jo. "Just one."

49

"Is it a spotty one?"

"A Gloucester Old Spots, d'you mean?"

"Yes," said Sophie. "I've seen them. At the Royal Wessex Agricultural Show. I'm going to be a lady farmer, you see. Is your pig one of those?"

"No," said Jo. "I'm just going to feed him. You can come too, if you like."

So Sophie plodded after her till they came to an old-fashioned brick-built pigsty, and there was the oddest-looking pig she had ever seen.

It was a dirty blackish colour, and very fat, with very short legs and a short wrinkled neck and a huge stomach that almost brushed the ground.

"Yikes!" said Sophie. "Whatever sort is that?"

"He's a Vietnamese pot-bellied pig," said Jo. "He's my special pet. My dad thought up a special Vietnamese name for him."

"What?" said Sophie.

"Mee-blong-jo," said Jo.

*　　*　　*

Sophie, now also smelling of pig, ate an enormous breakfast, and then the family piled into the car and set off for the sea.

The beach was wide and sandy, with rocks to climb and pools to paddle in, and the sea was calm, and there weren't too many people about, and the sun shone in a cloudless sky.

They all swam, including Puddle, of course, and it was easier in the sea, Sophie found. Matthew and Mark went off with a football and in no time at all they had found some other boys and started a game. And Sophie's mum and dad lay in the sun.

Sophie made a sandcastle, except that it was really a sand-farmhouse, with a sand-cowshed and a sand-pigsty, and altogether everything was lovely.

"Happy, Sophie?" they said, and Sophie nodded.

I am, she thought. I like being on the beach

and bathing, and I like my little bedroom, and Jo, she's all right, and Mee-blong-jo, he's mega, and I don't see what could spoil this holiday.

She got up from her building and called Puddle.

"I'm going for a walk along the beach," she said, "to get some shells."

"Not too far," they said. "Not out of our sight."

"OK," Sophie said.

She had not gone far when she came to a biggish rock that stuck up in the beach. Some people were sitting on the far side of this rock, a mother and father and a girl, and as Sophie approached, the girl got up and ran down towards the water.

She was a long-legged girl in a bright pink bathing-dress and her golden hair was done in bunches, tied with green ribbon.

It was Dawn.

Bumblebee

Sophie plodded back with a face like thunder. She arrived at the same time as the twins, who came racing up and threw themselves across an imaginary finishing-line, completely destroying Sophie's sand-farm. Sophie didn't even notice.

"Guess who I've just seen," she said in tones of deepest gloom.

"Haven't a clue," said her father.

"Someone from school," said Sophie.

"Someone you don't much like, by the look

of you," said her mother.

"I know!" said Mark.

"I know what you're going to say!" said Matthew.

"Dawn!" they shouted.

"Oh, no!" said her parents.

"Oh, yes," said Sophie. "She's just along the beach, with her horrible mum and her horrible dad."

"How d'you know they're horrible?"

"Well, they had Dawn, didn't they?"

"I think you should try to be nicer to poor Dawn," said Sophie's mother. "She can't be all that bad."

"Yuk!" said Sophie.

Long, long ago Dawn had deliberately squashed one of the largest of Sophie's herd of woodlice, and Sophie had neither forgotten nor forgiven.

The twins looked slyly at one another and grinned.

"Now you've got someone to play with," they said with one voice. Sophie turned an angry face upon them, and then saw the wreck of her sand-farm.

"Look what you've done!" she shouted. "You're mowldy, stupid and assive, you are!" and she charged furiously at them, but they ran away laughing.

"Calm down, Sophie," said her father. "I'll help you build another one."

"I don't want to build another one."

"Well, let's go and have another bathe."

"I don't want another bathe."

"Or throw sticks into the sea for Puddle."

"Don't want to."

"Well, what do you want then?"

"I want to go back to the farm."

"Not yet," said her father. "This weather's too good to miss. We shan't be going for hours yet."

"Cheer up, Sophie darling," said her mother. "Let's have our picnic lunch."

"Not hungry," said Sophie.

But in fact she found she was, and she was still eating when everyone else was full. And afterwards, Matthew and Mark helped her to build a simply enormous sandcastle and dug tunnels through it and decorated it with seaweed and shells and pebbles, and finally wrote in the sand with a piece of driftwood:

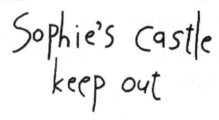

Sophie's castle
keep out

"And put 'Trespassers will be persecuted'," said Sophie.

"Prosecuted," said her father.

"Yes, and prosecuted too," said Sophie. "Like that Dawn ought to be, for coming on our beach."

This gave her an idea, and she took the piece of driftwood and went along to the big sticking-up rock, cautiously, in case they were still there. But they weren't, so Sophie wrote in the sand in huge letters:

Go hom Dawn

That'll scare her, she thought. She never saw me so it'll be really spooky for her to see her name there tomorrow; and at the end of the day Sophie

went home much happier, while the incoming tide crept up the beach and washed out her message.

By bedtime Sophie had quite recovered her spirits. She had been allowed to feed Mee-blong-jo, she had helped pick up the eggs in the henhouse, she had spoken to some sheep and chatted to some cows, and finally Jo had taken her round the stables and showed her some of the ponies, for the next day Sophie was to have her first riding lesson.

"I expect my mum will put you up on this one," Jo said, stroking the velvety muzzle of a grey pony that was looking out over the half-door of its box. "She's called Bumblebee. She's a beginner's pony."

"She's got a nice face," said Sophie.

"She's as quiet as an old sheep," said Jo.

*   *   *

"She's as quiet as an old sheep," said Jo's mother the next morning as she saddled up Bumblebee.

Sophie's father and the twins had gone to the beach, while her mother stayed behind to watch the first lesson.

"Only one thing Bumblebee doesn't like," said the farmer's wife, "and that's pigs. Which is one reason why we don't keep any, apart from that ugly old creature of Jo's."

"Why doesn't she like pigs?" asked Sophie.

A person who didn't like pigs would be foolish, she thought, so perhaps this was a foolish horse.

"Some horses are funny about things," the farmer's wife said. "We had a pony that was frightened stiff of the local bus – go mad, he would, if the bus came along. And another that hated going through gateways. Bumblebee, she

can't stand pigs. Now then, Sophie, ever been on
a horse before?"

"No," said Sophie, "but I'm going to be a lady
farmer, so I shall have to know how to ride a horse
round my flocks and herds."

"A lady farmer, eh? Not going to have a man
about the place, then?"

"I might," said Sophie. "I might marry Andrew,
but only if he's got a farm. If he hasn't, I shan't."

"You bain't so green as you'm cabbage-looking,
as we say round these parts," said the farmer's wife.
"Now then, let's get you up. You're not nervous,
are you?"

"No," said Sophie. She was, a tiny bit, but
she wasn't going to say so. All the same it felt
very odd once she was sitting on Bumblebee's
back. The pony was not a big one, but it did seem

to Sophie that she was rather a long way from the ground.

Jo's mother showed her how to hold the reins, and how her feet should be in the irons ("toes to Heaven, heels to Hell"), and told her to sit up straight and to keep her hands low. Then she said, "Now, all we're going to do is to walk along nice and quiet, with me holding the leading-rein. Ready?"

"Just a minute," said Sophie's mother, and she got out her camera to take a picture of stocky Sophie sitting on stocky Bumblebee.

"Cheese, Sophie!" she cried, but Sophie's face was grimly determined under the hard hat.

"That cap I gave her looks a bit small," the farmer's wife said. "Jo's would fit her better, I think," and she called, "Jo!"

"Yes?" came a voice from the far side of the yard.

"Can you come here a minute, please? Quickly."

Jo was in the pigsty, scratching the bristly back of her Vietnamese pot-bellied pet, who had lowered himself a few inches to lie blissfully on his fat stomach.

"Stay there, Mee-blong-jo," she said. "Shan't be half a tick," and she ran out of the sty. She pulled the door to but did not bother to latch it. Slowly, it swung open again.

The procession had only just started out – the farmer's wife, leading Bumblebee, Sophie, now wearing Jo's hat, sitting as straight as a ramrod, her mother walking behind – when round the corner came the small, fat, bristly black shape of Mee-blong-jo, squeaking happily to himself at this unexpected freedom.

Bumblebee let out a shrill neigh
of horror and shied violently, and
Sophie came off with a thump.

Her mother rushed to her.

"It's all right, darling," she said. "Don't cry."

"I'm not," said Sophie.

Sophie did not approve of crying.

"Get that pig of yours out of here, Jo!" shouted
the farmer's wife angrily, and to Sophie she said,
"Have you hurt yourself?"

"No," said Sophie. She had, a tiny bit, but she
wasn't going to say so.

"Perhaps we'd better leave it at that for today,"
her mother said.

"No," said Sophie. "I want to have another go."

"She's quite right," said the farmer's wife. She
lowered her voice. "Best thing to do, get straight on
again," she murmured. "Otherwise she might lose
her nerve."

Sophie's mother smiled.

"Not Sophie," she said.

"Come on, then," said the farmer's wife. "Up we go."

"Can I say something to Bumblebee first?" Sophie asked.

"Of course, if you want to."

Sophie plodded round and reached up to the grey pony's head and stroked her nose.

"Now then, my dear," she said. "You listen to me. The P-I-G has gone, so there's no need to be frightened any more."

"I thought I'd better spell it," she said, once she was astride again. "You never know how much animals can understand."

"No doubt about it," said the farmer's wife to Sophie's mother. "She's going to be a proper lady farmer, she is. Walk on!"

The Rescue

Sophie's words seemed to have calmed Bumblebee, who was as quiet and sheeplike as you could wish for the rest of the ride.

Afterwards Sophie's mother found her standing with her back to a long looking-glass, peering round at her reflection.

"Whatever are you doing?" she asked.

"Jo's mum said I had a good seat," said Sophie, "so I was just looking at it."

Her mother laughed.

"She meant
you sat naturally on
a horse," she said, "and
so you did. Some people ride
like sacks of potatoes, but I think
you're going to be a good horsewoman."

"Horsechild," said Sophie.

"How did you get on?" her father said when
he came back.

"I got off," said Sophie.

"She fell off," said her mother, "but she got
straight on again."

70

"That's my girl," said Sophie's father. "Small you
may be, but determined you certainly are."

After that the holiday developed a pattern. Sophie
had her riding lessons first thing after breakfast, and
then they all spent the day together on the beach.

At first Sophie had tried to persuade them to go
to a different, Dawn-free beach, but they said no,
this was the nicest and the nearest and anyway
with a bit of luck Dawn and her parents might go
somewhere else.

Which they must have done, because although
Sophie went off scouting each morning along
the sands – in disguise, that is to say wearing her
mother's dark glasses and with a sunhat pulled
well down – there was no sign of them.

"She must have read my notice," said Sophie
to Puddle.

Puddle was blissfully happy. Everything about the holiday suited him down to the ground. At night he slept in Sophie's room, supposedly in his basket but actually on her bed. Then there was the farm, with all its exciting sounds and smells, and his friends, the two collies. And lastly there was the sea, that lovely great watery paradise into which he plunged on any excuse and in which he swam tirelessly about, looking, with that black patch over one eye, the perfect pirate dog.

In general, he behaved very well, but he did have one bad habit. He would stand in front of anyone on the beach who was playing with a ball or a Frisbee, and yap at them.

What he was saying was as plain as could be.

"My family aren't throwing sticks for me just at the moment, so why don't you throw that ball or

that Frisbee, and I'll bring it back to you and we
can have a lovely game?"

Very occasionally some stranger would take
notice of this request, but mostly people told him
to buzz off, or else someone in Sophie's family
would call him back to them.

But one morning in the second week of the
holiday Puddle had wandered a little further than
usual along the beach, when he came upon a girl
in a bright pink bathing-dress, with golden hair
done in bunches, tied with green ribbon.

Dawn was sitting on the sand, midway between
the big sticking-up rock where her parents were,
and the sea. She was playing with a Sindy doll that
was almost a miniature of herself, bunches and all,
and Puddle rushed up to her with a volley of barks
that said, "Chuck it for me! Go on, chuck it, and

I'll bring it back, or I might chew it a bit, it looks good enough to chew. Go on, chuck it!"

Dawn was terrified. She was nervous of dogs anyway, and now suddenly out of nowhere had come this strange, noisy, piratical terrier, whose mouth, every yap showed, was full of sharp white teeth. She leapt to her feet and fled.

For Puddle this all added to the fun, and he gave chase, bouncing like a rubber ball beside her and snapping at the Sindy doll, till Dawn, bleating "Mummy! Daddy! Help!" tripped and fell.

At this point Sophie appeared, plodding along in search of Puddle, only to see him apparently attacking a fallen child.

Then everything happened at once.

Puddle, trying madly to grab the doll in his jaws, suddenly received a hefty slap from Sophie and

heard a furious shout of "Stop that, you bad dog, and get away!" and ran off.

Dawn's mother and father, rushing to the rescue, saw only that their precious daughter had been saved from a savage dog-attack by a stocky, dark-haired and apparently fearless little girl.

And Dawn, once she had stopped howling, saw Sophie. Sophie's face was a picture.

Fancy going to the help of that wimp Dawn! If only she'd realized in time she wouldn't have slapped poor Puddle, she'd have encouraged him. All he was trying to do was to chew up that revolting Sindy doll.

She turned to go back and make it up with the now distant Puddle, when Dawn's father said, "That was very brave of you, young lady."

"Brave?" said Sophie.

"Yes, rescuing my little girl from that vicious dog."

"He's not..." began Sophie, at the same time as Dawn said to her mother, "It's Sophie. From school."

"Sophie?" said Dawn's mother in horrified tones, remembering their first meeting when, after the squashing of the woodlouse, Sophie had taken Dawn's toy pony Twinkletoes and solemnly jumped up and down on it until it was a dirty squashed lump.

"From the same school, are you?" said Dawn's father. "Well, well! It's a small world! Fancy you two friends meeting so far from home!"

"She's not..." began Dawn and Sophie at the same time, but Dawn's father, who obviously liked the sound of his own voice, continued.

"Now then, young lady, we're very grateful to you

for what you did. Our Dawn might have been badly bitten by that nasty, vicious brute, and so might you."

"But…" said Sophie.

"No buts," said Dawn's father, and he put his hand in the pocket of his shorts and took out two one pound coins and held them out to Sophie.

"Here," he said, "I should like you to accept these – they'll buy you a few ice-creams – and once again, many thanks for what you did."

"Yes, thank you," said Dawn's mother, rather unwillingly. "Dawn, what do you say to Sophie?"

"Thank you," said Dawn, very unwillingly.

Sophie took the coins. She opened her mouth and then shut it again. Then she said "Thanks" and plodded off.

* * *

Afterwards everyone fell about laughing when she told them what had happened.

"Dawn's father gave you two quid?" cried Matthew.

"For rescuing her from Puddle?" cried Mark.

"But surely he wasn't trying to bite her?" said Sophie's mother.

"No, he was trying to get her beastly Sindy doll."

"Tell us again," said her father, "what they called him."

"A nasty, vicious brute," said Sophie.

She cuddled Puddle.

"You are a very good boy," she said, "and I'm sorry I slapped you."

"Talk about getting money under false pretences!" said her father. "You really should have told them he was your dog."

"He isn't. He's ours."

"Well, ours then."

"I tried," said Sophie, "but they wouldn't listen. So I thought, well, that's another two pounds for my Farm Money. Every little helps."

"As the old lady said," added Matthew.

"When she peed in the sea," ended Mark.

A Red-letter Day

The next day was wet, so they drove to the nearest large town. They went into a big department store, partly to get out of the rain, partly – even if they didn't buy anything – to have something to eat and drink in its café, and partly because the children liked riding up and down on the escalators.

Not surprisingly, Sophie's method of travel was not the same as the twins'. They ran up the Up escalators and down the Down, racing one another as always, while Sophie stood stock-still, feet together, on one step, enjoying the sensation of being lifted or dropped without any effort on her part.

At one point, Matthew and Mark stood at the bottom of a Down escalator, looking up as the steps fell towards them.

"I know!" said Mark.

"I know what you're going to say!" said Matthew.

"And so do I," said their father, "and the answer is most certainly No. You are not going to try to run up the Down one, or down the Up one for that matter. It's not allowed and it would be very dangerous, so forget it."

There were notices everywhere in the store, telling people where different things were sold. One, Sophie saw, said:

MENSWEAR

She did not comment on this, but a little later they came upon:

CHILDRENSWEAR

Sophie pointed at it.

"They shouldn't," she said.

"Who shouldn't?"

"Children shouldn't."

"Shouldn't what?"

"Swear," said Sophie.

They all laughed at that.

"Oh, Sophie!" her mother said. "You are a hoot!"

Sophie was not sure what a hoot was, and she did not like being laughed at in what she thought was a mowldy, stupid and assive way. So she hunched her shoulders and stumped along behind, scowling. But two jam doughnuts and a large chocolate ice-cream in the café cheered her up a bit.

"Only three more days left," her father said, stirring his coffee.

"And we still haven't sent a single postcard to any of our family or friends," said her mother. "It's always the same – we never remember until we're almost home again."

So then they went to the Stationery Department and chose their own cards.

Sophie was looking for two – one to send to Aunt Al up on top of the Highlands, and one to send to Tomboy and Beano at home.

Aunt Al's was easy – Sophie found a picture of a big black cat that she was sure must be the spitting image of Ollie – but it was more difficult to find a card that would suit both her own cat *and* Beano.

At last she did. It was a picture of a fieldmouse (which Tomboy would like) sitting amongst some nice green grass (which Beano would like).

Back at the farm, she wrote them.

On the one for Tomboy and Beano she just put:

Love from Sophie

"No use putting a lot of stuff on it," she said. "After all, they can't read."

With Aunt Al's she took more trouble:

We are staying on a farm
and I am having riding lessons
and I love them and tomorow
I am going to lern to jump.
lots of love to you and Ollie
from Sophie

Sophie's riding lessons had gone very well. Free from the menace of Mee-blong-jo, Bumblebee had behaved perfectly, and soon there had been no further need of the leading-rein. Sophie had learned to stop and start and steer the grey pony, and to rise to the trot, and had even managed a gentle controlled canter.

But she wanted more. She saw Jo (an experienced horsechild) take her own pony, Nipper, over the course of jumps set out round the paddock, and Jo made it look so easy.

"Can I have a jump?" she asked Jo's mother.

"It's early days for that, I think, Sophie," Jo's mother said.

"Perhaps next year, if you come again, which I hope you will."

Sophie looked so downcast that Jo's mother said,

"Perhaps tomorrow we'll let you have a try at a very little jump."

That tomorrow had been the rainy day, but at the end of it Sophie went to bed thinking that next morning she would not just ride round, but actually leap over an obstacle.

"Like a swallow," she said to Puddle, "because I have a natural seat and when I grow up I'm going to be a very good horsewoman and I shall probably win Badminton."

If Puddle could have understood and answered this, he would probably have said "Oh, yeah? And I'll be Supreme Champion at Crufts," but as it was, he just jumped up on the bed and they went to sleep.

Sophie's father usually settled down with his pipe and a newspaper during the hour's riding lesson after breakfast, while the twins kicked a football about on the farmhouse lawn, but on this day Sophie wasn't having that.

"You've all got to come and watch this morning," she said. "I'm going to jump Bumblebee."

"Jump over her, d'you mean?" said Matthew.

"Jump on top of her like you jumped on Dawn's Twinkletoes?" said Mark.

"Don't tease, boys," said their mother. "You'll be surprised how well Sophie's riding has come on."

They were, too. They all came – Jo and her father as well – and watched as Jo's mother put Sophie. and Bumblebee through their paces.

"Isn't it odd?" said Sophie's father to his wife. "No one could say that Sophie was exactly graceful on the ground, or athletic like the boys. She's more of a plodder. Yet she looks really good on that pony."

Not only did Sophie look good, she performed perfectly.

To be sure, the first jump she was asked to tackle was just a pole laid on the ground, which Bumblebee hopped over, but Sophie looked as proud as if it had been a five-barred gate.

And then Jo's mum put the pole up on some bricks so that it was a foot off the ground, and they jumped it beautifully, and everybody clapped.

"You were really good, Sophie," said her father afterwards.

"Not as good as Jo is."

"Well, she's been at it much longer."

"She's lucky, Jo is," Sophie said.

"Living on a farm, you mean?"

"Yes. But specially having a pony of her own. Daddy, d'you think…?"

"No, Sophie love," said her father. "You have a cat and a rabbit and one-fifth of a dog, but you are *not* having a pony."

"OK," said Sophie. "I just thought I'd ask."

The last morning of the seaside holiday came and a beautiful one it was. They had had good weather all along except for the one wet day, but this one was perfect – hot, but not too hot, and cloudless, with a nice breeze off a sunlit sea.

Sophie had her final riding lesson, and jumped Bumblebee over a pole that was a good two feet off the ground. Then they drove down to the beach, and bathed, and played, and had a lovely picnic, and never saw hide nor hair of Dawn.

And to cap it all, in the afternoon, Sophie's father hired a boat, and a nice old Cornish fisherman took them out into the bay, and Puddle jumped overboard and had to be rescued. They put out some lines for mackerel but didn't catch anything, which Sophie was glad about. Partly this was because she thought it must be very painful to have a little hook in your mouth, and partly because she was worried they might catch a pilchard, which (in tomato sauce) was her most unfavourite food.

And afterwards, when the old fisherman put

them ashore, he shook hands with everyone in turn.

When he came to Sophie he said, "And how
old be you, m'dear?"

"Six," said Sophie.

The old fisherman smiled down at her.

"Next summer," he said, "when you do come
back to Cornwall, you'll be growed up
like a runner bean."

Afterwards Sophie said,
"Shall we come back
next summer?"

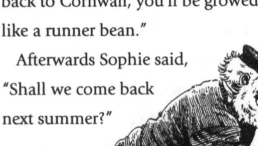

"Let's!" said the twins.

"We might," said their mother.

"We'll see," said their father.

The next morning, while the car was being packed up, Sophie went round with Jo to say goodbye – to the cows and the sheep and the hens and the ducks and the geese, and to Mee-blong-jo, and to Nipper and the other horses and ponies, and, last of all, to Bumblebee.

"Goodbye, my dear," she said to the grey pony. "Be good, and keep away from that P-I-G, and I'll see you in a year."

"It's an awful long time to wait," she said to Jo.

"Isn't there a riding school near where you live?" Jo said.

"I expect so," said Sophie.

"Well, you ought to go on with your lessons. You're going to be good, Mum says so. Then next year you'd be able to ride really well and go over all these jumps – you could ride my Nipper if you like."

"Gosh, thanks," said Sophie. "But I've only got twelve pounds and seventy pence Farm Money, and riding lessons are sure to be expensive."

"Ask your mum and dad."

"They'll say 'Wait till next summer'."

"Riding lessons are expensive," they said when Sophie asked them. "Wait till next summer."

Sophie felt sad as they drove away, sad at leaving Jo and her mum and dad and all the animals, sad at leaving the sea in which she and Puddle had doggy-paddled about so happily.

Then she went to sleep.

When she woke up again they were almost home, and then very soon she was stroking Tomboy and petting Beano, and unpacking in her own room with the pictures of Blossom and April and May and Shorty and Measles.

"Sophie!" her mother called from downstairs. "There's a letter for you."

Sophie plodded downstairs, frowning in thought.

Who could it be from?

She looked at the handwriting on the envelope. It seemed familiar.

She looked at the postmark. DRUMOCHTER, it said.

She opened the envelope.

Dear Sophie,

Thanks for your postcard. Glad you are having a nice time. I am well and so is Ollie. Interested to hear you are learning to ride. I was pretty good on a horse seventy-five years ago.

Love from Aunt Al

P.S. Why not get your mother and father to find out if there's a good riding school near you where you could have a course of lessons? It would make a nice combined Christmas and seventh birthday present, wouldn't it?

P.T.O.

They wouldn't pay for a course of lessons, Sophie thought. It's too expensive, they said so.

"What does P.T.O. mean?" she said.

"Please Turn Over."

Sophie turned over the page of writing paper, and read:

P.P.S. A present from me, I meant.

A.A.

and from Sophie there came a great cry of "YIKES!"

Sophie
Is Seven

Contents

Sophie in
the Garden

One day in late autumn Sophie sat on the edge
of her bed, holding her piggy-bank. She had
just stuck a fresh label on its side. The first label,
when she was only four, had said:

Farm munny
thank you
Sophie

Later, she had crossed out MUNNY and written MONNEY instead, and now, getting on for seven, she had designed a new label that read:

Farm Money. Please Give Genrusly. Thank You. Sophie

Sophie unscrewed the plug in the pig's stomach and tipped out the contents and counted them. They came to twelve pounds, seventy pence.

She looked round the walls of her bedroom at the pictures, drawn by her mother, of a cow called Blossom, two hens called April and May, a spotty pig named Measles and a pony named Shorty.

These were the animals she would buy once she became a lady farmer. Sophie, though very small, was very determined, and no one in the family doubted that she would one day achieve her ambition.

Now she rubbed the tip of her nose, a sign that she was thinking deeply.

"Twelve pounds, seventy," said Sophie, "is not enough. I shall have to raise some more money, somehow."

At that moment her twin brothers Matthew and Mark burst into the room. Matthew was ten minutes older than Mark, and both were two and a bit years older than Sophie, and neither of them ever walked when he could run or spoke quietly when he could shout.

"Wow!" they cried with one voice, at the sight of the money spread upon Sophie's bed. "How much have you got?"

"Twelve pounds, seventy," said Sophie, "and where are your manners?"

"What d'you mean?" they said.

"You should knock before you come into a lady's bedroom. You're rude, you are."

"And mowldy," said Matthew.

"And stupid," said Mark.

"And assive," they both said, for this was how an angry Sophie had always described them.

They grinned at one another.

"I know!" said Mark.

"I know what you're going to say!" said Matthew.

"And so do I," said Sophie, "and the answer is NO. I am not going to lend you any money, not one penny."

"Meanie!" they cried, and off they dashed, racing one another down the stairs.

Sophie put all the money back in the piggy-
bank and screwed up its stomach again. Then she
plodded downstairs and stood it on the hall table,
where anyone who came to the house would,
she hoped, read its message. Then she went to find
her mother.

"Mum," she said. "How do you raise money?"

"For a good cause, d'you mean?" her mother said.

"Yes. A very good one."

"Like Children in Need, that sort of thing?"

"Yes," said Sophie.

I am a child in need, she thought.

"Well, there are all sorts of ways. You can have
jumble sales, or raffles, or things like sponsored
walks."

"What's that mean?" asked Sophie.

"Well, people set out to walk a certain distance –

ten miles, let's say – and other people agree to pay a sum of money for each mile they manage to go. Twenty pence a mile, perhaps."

"Or one pound a mile?" said Sophie.

"Possibly."

"That'd be ten pounds."

"Yes, and if you persuaded ten people to sponsor you at one pound a mile, and then you walked ten miles, that'd be a hundred pounds for the good cause."

"Yikes!" said Sophie softly.

Ten miles, she thought. I bet I could walk ten miles. It's not like a marathon, you don't have to run.

Later she said to the twins, "How far is a marathon?"

"Twenty-six miles," said Matthew.

"And three hundred and eighty-five yards," said Mark.

Sophie went off to the potting-shed where once she had kept her flocks and herds of snails and slugs and centipedes and suchlike creatures. Now only her white rabbit Beano lived there in his large hutch.

Sophie discussed the matter with him.

"Just walking ten miles is easier than running more than twenty-six, wouldn't you say, my dear?" she asked him. "Miles easier."

Beano, a large rabbit with floppy ears, stared at her with his red eyes. He had a wiffly nose, and now he wiffled it at Sophie, in agreement, she thought.

Then Sophie's black cat Tomboy poked her nose around the door of the shed.

"I could walk ten miles," Sophie said. "Couldn't I, Tomboy?"

"*Nee-o*," said the cat, or that was what it sounded like. Sophie looked out at the garden. It was a rough square in shape, and there was a gravelled path that ran right round it. Sophie plodded right round it, once.

"I wonder how far that was," she said.

That evening she asked her father, "Daddy, how far is it round our garden?"

"Round the path, d'you mean?"

"Yes. Half a mile, d'you think?"

Sophie's father laughed.

"I'll pace it out for you if you like," he said. "My step is about a yard long. Why d'you want to know, anyway?"

"I just do," Sophie said.

So her father walked solemnly round all four sides of the garden, counting aloud.

"Eighty-nine," he said at the end. "Call it eighty-eight, it makes it easier, because then ten times round would be eight hundred and eighty yards, or half a mile."

"Yikes!" said Sophie. "So if you wanted to walk a mile, you'd have to go round..." She paused for thought.

"Twenty times!" her father said.

"What if someone wanted to walk ten miles?"

"Two hundred times. If anyone was mad enough to do it. Satisfied now? Because I want to go in and watch the cricket on TV."

Two hundred times, Sophie thought. Still, I bet I could do that.

In the sitting-room she found Matthew and Mark,

who were keen on all sport, also watching the cricket. Puddle, the family's dog, a small white terrier with a black patch over his right eye, sat in front of the television set, quivering with eagerness. One thing he loved was chasing a ball, and he could see one there, being bowled or thrown or hit. Just let it come out of that box and he'd have it! Sophie stared at the screen absently, her mind full of this scheme – so simple, it seemed – for raising money.

Suppose Daddy gave a pound for each mile, and Mum another one, and the twins – no, more likely they'd give a penny. She'd have to get a lot of other people to pay, so as to raise a lot more Farm Money. Like everyone at school perhaps. Except Dawn, of course. Dawn was a girl with whom Sophie had often tangled in the past and she would certainly not give anything at all.

Still, the first thing to be done was to walk the ten miles. Then she could tell everybody she'd done it and then they'd pay up. First thing tomorrow, said Sophie to herself, I'll do it. Now, that decided, she paid some attention to the cricket. After a bit she said, "It looks nice and sunny where they're playing, so why is that man wearing a hat and a white coat, with a sweater round his neck and another sweater tied round his middle? Is he cold?"

"No," they all said. "He's one of the umpires."

"The bowlers take off their sweaters to bowl," said Mark.

"And he looks after them," said Matthew.

"What a nice man," said Sophie.

A little later she said, "Why's he doing that?"

"Who?" said Matthew.

"The empire."

"Umpire," said Mark. "Doing what?"

"Taking something out of one of his pockets and putting it in the other one."

"Those are pebbles," said her father. "He's counting how many balls the bowler's bowled. When he's transferred six pebbles from one pocket to the other, he says 'Over'."

"Why?" said Sophie.

"It's the end of the over. Then everyone changes ends. They all cross over."

"Over what?" said Sophie.

"Oh, do be quiet, Sophie," said the twins.

"Just watch for a bit, Sophie," said her father, "and you may get the hang of it."

"No, I won't," said Sophie, and she stumped off, scowling.

By the time Sophie went to bed that night her

plans were laid. First thing tomorrow she would do that ten-mile walk. Going round the garden two hundred times was sure to take quite a while, so, she thought, I must make an early start. She banged her head on the pillow six times, and went straight to sleep.

When she woke, she looked at her watch and saw to her surprise that it was indeed exactly six o'clock.

Sophie dressed quickly, crept downstairs, put on her wellies, and went out, Puddle at her heels, into a damp, overcast morning.

"We'll start by the potting-shed, my dear," she said to Puddle, "and when we come round to it for the two hundredth time, that'll be it. Simple. Except we'll have to keep count or we might go round too many times."

"Got it!" she said, and she bent and picked up
a handful of bits of gravel from the path and put
them in the pocket of her jeans. Then she opened
the potting-shed door, said "Good morning"
to Beano, gave him a carrot, and found an old
cardboard box which had BAKED BEANS in black
print on one side and on the other SNALES in big
red capitals.

She put the box down in the doorway and set off
around the garden path, Puddle following. As she
passed the potting-shed after the first circuit, she
took a piece of gravel from her pocket and dropped
it into the cardboard box.

"Only a hundred and ninety-nine to go!" said
Sophie to Beano, and plodded on. From the leaden
sky a few large drops began to fall.

At half past six Sophie's mother was woken by

the rattle of raindrops against her window-pane.

She got out of bed without disturbing her sleeping husband and went to look out into the garden. It needs rain, she thought. There below her was Sophie, plodding solemnly around the garden path in the steady downpour.

As her mother watched in amazement, she reached the open door of the potting-shed, took something from her pocket, threw it into a box, and stumped on, Puddle trotting after.

Sophie's mother hurried downstairs, threw a macintosh over her nightclothes and ran for the potting-shed through the teeming rain. Hardly had she reached its shelter than Sophie appeared again outside its door, a piece of gravel in her hand.

"Sophie!" her mother cried. "Come inside here straight away!"

Sophie came into the shed. Her dark hair, which always looked as though she had just come through a hedge backwards, now looked as if she had just swum the Channel. It was plastered to her head, and her clothes – old jeans and an old much-too-small blue jersey with her name written on it in white letters – were sopping wet. Her wellies squelched. Puddle, who loved water, came in too and shook himself happily over them.

"What in the world have you been doing?" Sophie's mother said.

"Walking," said Sophie shortly.

"In all this rain? Round and round the garden path? Why?"

"To raise money. For a good cause. Like you said."

"A sponsored walk, you mean?"

Sophie nodded, dripping.

"What were you trying to raise money for?"

"My farm," said Sophie. "I've only got twelve pounds, seventy."

Her mother looked fondly at her small but determined daughter.

"Come into the house," she said, "and we'll get those wet things off and put you in a nice hot bath."

"But I haven't finished my walk," Sophie said.

"Yes, you have. Come on."

"Oh, all right then," Sophie said. "Just wait half

a minute," and she began to count the pieces
of gravel in the SNALES box.

"Twenty," she said.

"You mean you've been round twenty times?"

"Yes. That's a mile, Dad said. I've still got nine
miles to do."

In the bath Sophie sat playing with a rubber frog
that squeaked. Puddle, rubbed dry now, sat on the
mat hopefully. Just let it hop out of that bath and
he'd have it!

"So how much money d'you think I'll get for
walking a mile?" Sophie said.

"Sophie love," said her mother gently. "You've
got things a bit muddled. A sponsored walk means
that you have to go round to everyone *before* you
do the walk and get them to sponsor you. *Then*

you do the walk, and then they pay up."

"Oh," said Sophie.

"And usually people walk a long way across country, not just round and round the garden."

"Oh," said Sophie. "So I shan't get anything?"

"Well," said her mother, "let's pretend that I did sponsor you. How far did you say you'd gone?"

"A mile."

"Then I'll give you one pound."

Sophie grinned.

"Thanks, Mum," she said. "Actually I was quite glad to stop. I did want to do ten miles but I don't think I'd have had the stanima."

"Stamina, you mean."

"Yes. Can we have breakfast now? I'm starved."

Sophie in
the Classroom

S ophie enjoyed school. She quite liked the
teachers – they were all right – and she did not
mind the other children (except Dawn), though
she did not make friends easily.

Partly this was because she was perfectly happy
on her own, and partly it was because a good
number of the other children were, in her opinion,
either wimps (like Dawn) or wallies (like Duncan,

a very small boy with ginger hair, short legs and a
fat stomach). At one point Sophie had considered
taking on Duncan as a farm labourer when she
should become a lady farmer, but later she had
sacked him.

She did, however, approve of one boy, Andrew,
a farmer's son, and she sometimes contrived to
go to tea at the farm (by telling Andrew to ask his
mother to ask her). Like Jo, a girl she had met on
a recent Cornish seaside holiday, Andrew smelled
nice to Sophie. Jo smelled of pig and horse,
Andrew of cow.

The only thing about school to which Sophie
objected was that they didn't have Farming
Lessons.

"I can't understand why they don't," she said.
"It's all very well to teach me to read and add up

and stuff like that, but how am I going to become a lady farmer if they don't teach me farming?"

"You have to be taught lots of other things first," said her father.

"And you've got plenty of books about farms," her mother said. "You could learn quite a bit from them."

"Or from Andrew," said Mark.

"Your boyfriend," said Matthew.

"He's not my boyfriend," said Sophie angrily. "He's my friend."

"Well, if he's your friend ..." said Matthew.

"... and he's a boy ..." said Mark.

"...then he's your boyfriend," they said.

"You," said Sophie, "are mowldy, stupid and assive!" and she stumped off.

But after half-term Sophie had a pleasant surprise.

On the first day back at school, her teacher said to the class, "Now then, children, the topic we are all going to do for the next few weeks is Farming."

"Yikes!" cried Sophie.

"I thought you would be pleased, Sophie," said the teacher, "and I expect you will be too, Andrew."

Andrew, a sturdy little boy of about Sophie's height and build, but with very fair, almost white, hair, said loftily, "I know all about farming already."

"How clever," said the teacher. "Then you'd better keep quiet for a minute while I ask the rest of the class some questions. Now then, where does milk come from?"

A forest of hands shot up.

"Well, Dawn?"

"Out of a bottle," said Dawn.

Sophie gave a snort.

Dawn looked to her even more revolting than usual. As well as the green bows with which her bunches of fair hair were always tied, she wore little gold earrings and her fingernails were painted coral pink.

"Well, Sophie," said the teacher, "is Dawn right?"

"She's ingerant," Sophie said.

"You mean ignorant."

"I mean soft in the head," said Sophie. "Milk comes out of a cow."

"She's right, you know," said Andrew.

"Yes, I daresay she is, but there's no need to be so rude to Dawn, Sophie. And anyway, since you know all about it, tell us why the cow has milk."

"To feed its baby of course," said Sophie. "All mothers do. I shall one day, after I'm married."

"Yes, yes," said the teacher. "Let's just stick to

cows for the moment. Now then, someone – not Sophie or Andrew – tell me, what is a cow's baby called?"

"A calf!" said several voices.

"You have to have a bull," said Sophie.

"She's right, you know," said Andrew.

"Yes, yes, quite right, Sophie," said the teacher hurriedly. "Now then, what other animals do farmers keep?"

The forest of hands sprouted again.

"Sheep," said someone.

"Pigs," said someone else.

"Horses," said Duncan, who had spent some time as a horse in the playground, being lunged on the end of a skipping-rope. At first he had been Sophie's horse, but later, when Sophie was away with chicken-pox, he had trotted around Dawn.

On Sophie's return that had all ended in tears (not Sophie's).

"Farmers don't have horses," said Andrew scornfully. "They have tractors. We've got a big green one. Cost half a million pounds, it did."

"I'm sure there are still a few farmers that use horses," the teacher said. "But you've all forgotten about some other creatures. What about birds? What sort of birds would a farmer keep?"

"Chickens," said someone.

"And ducks and geese," said someone else.

"Ostriches," said Sophie.

There were giggles and sniggers, especially from Dawn.

"Don't be silly, Sophie," said the teacher.

Sophie's face darkened.

"They do," she said. "They do have ostrich farms,

I saw it on the telly."

"She's right, you know," said Andrew.

"Just be quiet, both of you," said the teacher.

"Now we've mentioned chickens and ducks and geese, but we've forgotten another sort of bird. A big one, it is."

"Ostriches are big," said Sophie.

"No, no, this is a bird that we connect with a very special day, not many weeks away now."

Everyone looked blank, so the teacher said, "The twenty-fifth of December. What's that?"

"My seventh birthday," said Sophie.

"Yes, yes, but what else?"

"Christmas Day!" said Dawn.

"Yes, so what bird am I talking about?"

"A turkey!"

"That's right. Everyone looks forward to

Christmas dinner, don't they?"

"No," said Sophie. "The turkeys don't."

"I'm beginning to think," said Sophie's teacher to the others as she drank her coffee in the staff room at break, "that I shouldn't have chosen Farming as a topic. I'm not quite sure who's teaching the class, me or Sophie and Andrew."

Later she set the children to draw and colour pictures, to make a display for the classroom walls.

"Choose something to do with farming," she said.

Most of them set to work to draw an animal of some kind, though Andrew began a picture of a very large tractor with a very small figure (himself) driving it, and began to colour it green.

The teacher approached Sophie's place somewhat nervously. I bet she's drawing an ostrich, she thought. Or a turkey, probably being chased by a man with an axe.

But in fact Sophie had drawn a very fat cow.

Beneath the exact centre of its huge belly was an enormous udder.

"Goodness!" said the teacher. "She must be a good milker."

"She is," said Sophie shortly.

The teacher pointed at the four large, stiff sausage shapes sticking out beneath the udder.

"Those are a bit big, aren't they?" she said.

"What, her tits?" said Sophie.

"Teats, they're called."

"Farmers call them tits," said Sophie.

"She's right, you know," said Andrew.

"That's where the milk comes out, you see," said Sophie.

"Yes, Sophie, I think we all know that."

"You can't be sure," said Sophie. "Some people are ingerant," and she pointed her pencil at Dawn.

Hastily the teacher said, "What are you going to call your cow, Sophie?"

"Blossom," said Sophie.

"That's a nice name. Though I still think you've drawn her rather too fat."

"Of course she is," said Sophie. "That's because she's just going to have a calf. I told you, didn't I? About the bull. Remember? Then nine months afterwards the cow gets very fat and very full of milk, see?"

"She's right, you know," said Andrew.

Sophie
at the Stables

"Mum?" said Sophie one Saturday morning.

"Yes?"

"When can I start having riding lessons?"

"Not till after Christmas. You remember Aunt Al's offer."

Sophie remembered all right. She had done some riding when they were on holiday in

Cornwall, and had loved it, and had told Aunt Al all about it.

Aunt Al was really Sophie's great-great-aunt, but they were also great, great friends. Though one was not yet seven and the other had just passed eighty-two, they were very much the same sort of person. Each was small and determined, and each took a no-nonsense approach to life's problems.

At the end of the holidays Aunt Al had offered to pay for Sophie to have riding lessons locally, as a combined Christmas and birthday present.

"It's a long time to wait," Sophie said now to her mother.

"Only a matter of weeks."

"But where shall I have the lessons?"

"At a riding school."

"But I don't know any."

"I expect there are lots round about. Look in the *Yellow Pages*."

Sophie plodded off and found the *Yellow Pages* directory and opened it in the middle of the Rs.

"Removals – Rest Homes – Restaurants – ah, here we are, Riding Schools," she said to Tomboy, who was snoozing on the sofa. She stroked her black back.

"I am going to learn to ride really properly, my dear," she said, "like a lady farmer should. Let's see if we can find one that's nice and near."

There were quite a number within easy distance of Sophie's home, but one particular advertisement caught her eye.

CLOVERLEA STABLES

- Children and beginners welcome
- Learn to ride and enjoy the freedom of the countryside
- Day, half-day or hourly
- Ponies for sale

Sophie looked at that last line. Just imagine, she thought.

"You never know," she said to Tomboy. "Once upon a time I didn't have an animal of my own. Then I got you, my dear, and then my own rabbit, and then my own dog," (for Sophie preferred to think of Puddle as hers, rather than the family's) "so how about my own pony?"

"*Neee-o*," said Tomboy.

"It might just fit in the potting-shed if it wasn't too fat, and riding round the garden two hundred times would be much easier than walking."

Sophie rubbed the tip of her nose. The twins had gone out with their father, she knew, and, looking out of the window, she saw that her mother was pruning her rose bushes. Sophie dialled the number of Cloverlea Stables.

"Have you a pony for sale, suitable for a child of nearly seven?" she said.

"You want to buy a pony?" said a woman's voice at the other end.

"Yes."

"As a matter of fact I have. Is it for a beginner?"

"Sort of," said Sophie.

"I've a very pretty little child's pony, a palomino mare, twelve hands, quiet as a lamb."

And not too fat, I hope, thought Sophie.

"How much?" she said.

"I couldn't take less than a thousand pounds."

"Oh," said Sophie. "I've only got thirteen pounds, seventy."

"Oh dear," said the woman. "That wouldn't even cover two riding lessons."

"Yikes!" said Sophie. "How much are they then?"

"Ten pounds an hour. That's with a small group of other children."

Sophie was silent. Aunt Al once gave me five pounds for my birthday, she thought, so I suppose she just might make it ten pounds this time. But that's only for an hour. How am I going to learn to ride really well in an hour?

"Are you still there?" asked the voice at the other end.

"Yes."

"Well, why not get your mummy or daddy to give me a ring? Then we can talk about it."

"OK," said Sophie. "You'd better not say anything about me wanting to buy a pony, if you don't mind."

"I won't say a word," said the woman.

"Thanks," said Sophie. "See you soon."

I hope, she thought as she put the phone down.
She went out to her mother.

"I phoned up a riding school," she said.

"Did you? Good. When you do start we must see
if they'll sell us a bag of horse manure. It'd do these
roses a power of good."

Buy me a pony, thought Sophie, and you
can have as much manure as you like, free.

"The lessons are very expensive," she said.

"How much?"

"Ten pounds an hour."

"I'm not surprised."

"Aunt Al will be," said Sophie.

"Perhaps you'd better
telephone her," said her
mother.

So Sophie did.

Aunt Al lived in the Highlands of Scotland, right on the very tip-top of them, Sophie always imagined, surrounded by golden eagles and blue hares and red deer.

Sophie had spoken to her on the phone several times before, and it always amazed her to think of her voice rushing along all those hundreds of miles of telephone wires and then finally right up the steep slopes of those very high Highlands, and then of Aunt Al's voice rushing all the way back down again. And all just as quick as if she was in the room, and as clear too.

"Hello, Aunt Al," she said. "It's me."

"Sophie!" said Aunt Al. "How nice to hear your voice. How's everyone?"

"Oh, Tomboy and Beano and Puddle are fine," said Sophie.

"I meant your parents really, and the boys."

"Oh, they're OK. How's Ollie?"

Ollie was Aunt Al's cat, a son of Tomboy.

"He's just fine. I'm fine too."

There was a pause while Sophie tried to decide how to break the news. She'll have a fit when she hears how much, she thought.

"Was there something special you were ringing up for?" said Aunt Al.

"Yes," said Sophie. She did not approve of beating about the bush, so now she came straight out with it.

"Those riding lessons you said you'd give me."

"Well?"

"They're ever so expensive."

"How much?"

"Ten pounds an hour."

All the way down that long line from the

Highlands came a long, low whistle.

"Are they indeed?" said Aunt Al.

"Yes," said Sophie. "So I'm just ringing up to say thank you very much but I don't think I could learn to ride really well in an hour so perhaps we'd better forget it."

"Load of rubbish!" said Aunt Al. "Now you listen to me, Sophie. If I remember rightly, I offered to pay for a course of riding lessons, as a combined Christmas and seventh birthday present. Didn't I?"

"Yes."

"Well, then a course of riding lessons is what you're going to have. Get it?"

"Yes."

"If you're going to learn to ride, then you're going to learn to ride properly, understand?"

"Yes."

"I did, when I was your age, and I've never regretted it. Just don't get any crack-brained ideas about having a pony of your own. It'd cost the earth to buy, let alone keep."

"Yes. Thanks, Aunt Al."

"Goodbye then."

"Goodbye."

So the next day Sophie went to Cloverlea Stables.

Her father was playing golf, and Matthew and Mark were playing football as usual, so Sophie's mother said to her, "Let's go and have a look at this riding school you phoned up. We want to make sure that Aunt Al's money is going to be well spent," and she rang up and fixed a time.

In the stable yard they got out of the car to see a number of faces looking out at them over the

half-doors of a row of loose-boxes. Then round the corner of the block came a large, tall lady, closely followed by a tortoiseshell-and-white cat.

Something about them both was familiar to Sophie.

The cat made straight for her and wound itself around her legs, tail stiffly upright, purring like a steam-engine.

"Well," said the large, tall lady, "Dolly seems to like you."

"Sophie's good with animals," her mother said.

"Sophie?" said the large, tall lady, and she looked hard at her.

"Dolly?" said Sophie, and she looked hard at the cat.

"Got it!" said the large, tall lady. "You're the little girl I bought Dolly from as a kitten. I remember

now, you just had the one queen. The others were all toms, and I seem to recall you were a bit miffed about that."

"I was," said Sophie. "I hoped they were all female and then I could have bred loads of kittens and sold them to make money for my farm."

"So you're going to be a farmer?"

"A lady farmer."

"Quite so," said the riding school owner, whose

name was Meg Morris. "In that case, learning to ride would be a good idea so that one day you can ride round your farm. Have you ever been on a pony before?"

"Yes," said Sophie. "Last summer. In Cornwall. He was called Bumblebee. I fell off once."

"But she got straight on again," said Sophie's mother, "and before the end of the holiday she actually hopped over some little jumps."

"Good," said Meg Morris. "Then I needn't treat her as an absolute beginner. When would you like her to start?"

"Today," said Sophie.

"After Christmas," said her mother.

"I couldn't fit you in yet anyway, Sophie," said the large, tall lady. "I'm pretty booked up. Let's have a look in the diary."

Inside an old stable that served as an office, Meg Morris said, "Now then, Christmas Day is on a Saturday this year, so the following Saturday will be New Year's Day, and it just so happens that I'm starting a new group then. Five is the maximum number I teach at one time, and I've already got four little girls booked, so Sophie would make five. How about that? Saturday, January the first, ten o'clock?"

"Fine," said Sophie's mother. "And now we must be off."

"Goodbye, Dolly, I must leave you," said Sophie, giving the tortoiseshell cat a final stroke.

"She's a wonderful mouser," said Meg Morris. "I can't remember what I paid you for her but she's been worth every penny of it."

"Five pounds," said Sophie, "and that reminds me."

She fished in her pocket and brought out the one pound coin that her mother had given her for the sponsored walk.

"Do you sell horse dung?" she said.

"Yes. There's some bagged up, at the other end of the yard."

"I want a bagful, please, for Mum's roses," said Sophie. "How much?"

"To you, Sophie," said the large, tall Meg Morris, "nothing. Take it as a present from Dolly and me."

"Thanks," said Sophie. "I'm very gracious." And she plodded off down the yard.

"She means 'grateful'," said her mother.

"She means well," said Meg Morris.

In the car on the way home Sophie's mother said, "That was very nice of you to think of buying me that manure."

"That's all right, Mum," Sophie said.

She twisted round to look at the bulging bag on the back seat.

"Yikes!" she said happily. "What a lovely pong! It's delirious!"

Sophie
on the Coach

No one entering Sophie's classroom could be in any doubt about what topic the children were doing.

The walls were covered with drawings and paintings of all things agricultural. As well as Sophie's hideous cow and Andrew's enormous tractor, there were flocks and herds of every animal you could possibly expect to see on an English farm. There were also several that you would have been surprised to come across (zebras, for example, and a solitary polar bear).

There were pictures of cowsheds and cornfields, of haystacks and henhouses, of duckponds and Dutch barns, and a great many pieces of descriptive writing about life on the farm.

There were also several poems, one of which was by Sophie.

Underneath a picture of a heap of tin cans and bottles, and car tyres, and an old TV set with a busted screen, she had written:

Do not be a litter lout
And throw your rubbish about
Always put your bottle or tin
In a rubbish bin
Another thing farmers hate
Is if you don't shut the gate
Because his animals will stray
And some will run away
And keep your dog on a lead
Or it may chase the sheep and make them bleed
If the farmer sees it he will shoot it
Because trespassers will be persecuted.

Underneath the poem was another picture, of a man with a smoking gun, a white sheep with red blobs all over it, and a very dead-looking dog lying on its back with its legs in the air.

"It's a very good poem, Sophie," her teacher had said.

"It is, isn't it," Sophie said.

"And it rhymes beautifully."

"It does, doesn't it."

"But could you shoot someone's dog like that, when you're a farmer, I mean?"

"A lady farmer," Sophie said. "No, I couldn't."

"Why not?"

"Lady farmers don't have guns."

"But suppose you did?"

"I still shan't shoot any dogs."

"Because you couldn't do such a thing, you mean?"

"No, because I shan't keep any sheep."

"I never seem to be able to get the better of
Sophie," said her teacher to the headmistress.

"You don't surprise me. How's your farming
project coming along?"

"Quite well, I think. If I go wrong, there's always
Sophie to put me right. Or Andrew."

"Let's see, it's tomorrow that you're taking your
class on a visit to a farm, isn't it?"

"Yes."

"Good luck."

Before the coach arrived, Sophie's teacher checked
to see that every child was wearing wellies (because
it would be mucky on the farm) and an anorak
(because it looked like rain). She made sure that

everyone had brought a lunch-box, and told them all that they were not to open them on the coach.

"You've only just had your breakfasts," she said, "so you can wait till midday."

On the coach the children sat in pairs, either side of the central gangway. Andrew sat with Sophie, because she had told him to. Opposite them, short fat Duncan plumped himself down beside tall thin Dawn. Dawn's parents spoiled her, always buying her lots of sweets, and Duncan, who was very greedy, knew that she would have a pocketful. Because he doubted that the contents of his lunch-box would be enough for him, he had secreted in his own anorak pocket a full packet of chocolate biscuits.

On the drive through the countryside the children gazed out of the windows of the coach with cries of, "Oh look, cows!" or, "There's a tractor!" For Sophie, the lady farmer, and Andrew, the farmer's son, this was not good enough, and they set the record straight by adding, "They're Friesians" or, "It's a John Deere."

Only Duncan was not interested in the passing scene. In between wheedling sweets from Dawn he was quietly stuffing himself with chocolate biscuits. The teacher, sitting right at the rear of the coach with a couple of mothers who had come along to help, did not notice. Sophie did.

She nudged Andrew and pointed across.

"I should think he'll make himself sick," she said.

Andrew nodded.

After a while the combination of the swaying coach and the sweets and biscuits began to take effect upon Duncan. He turned pale and shifted uncomfortably in his seat.

"He's going to be sick soon," said Sophie.

Andrew nodded.

Then there was a groan from Duncan and a squeal from Dawn.

"Yuk!" said Sophie. "He's been sick."

"And how!" said Andrew.

"What's all the fuss about?" called the teacher.

"Duncan's been sick on Dawn," said Sophie.

The teacher, experienced in coach trips, had brought with her a bucket, a cloth and a roll of kitchen paper. Armed with these, she came hurrying down the gangway.

"It's OK," Sophie said. "He did it over her wellies."

"My new wellies!" wailed Dawn, for they

had indeed been shiningly new and of a horrid pink colour.

The teacher looked at Duncan, who was pale green.

"Did you open your lunch-box?" she asked.

Duncan shook his head.

"No," he said truthfully.

After she had mopped up, the teacher found the lunch-box and looked inside it. It was crammed full of food.

"Have you been giving him something, Dawn?" the teacher asked. Dawn shook her head.

"No," she lied.

The teacher turned to Sophie opposite.

"Did you see Duncan eating?" she said.

Sophie did not approve of telling lies.

"Yes," she said.

"Was Dawn feeding him?"

But Sophie also did not approve of telling tales, so she did not answer.

"Was she, Andrew?"

"Yes," said Andrew, "she was giving him sweets and he was eating chocolate biscuits and they never offered none of them to us, not neither of them. They're greedy, they are."

"It's enough to make you sick," said Sophie.

The farm to which they were going was one that was regularly visited by parties of schoolchildren, and the farmer's wife was waiting, ready to show them round.

The first thing she did was to give each child a little paper bag full of corn, to feed to all the many hens and ducks and geese, not to mention a number of piglets, that were ranging freely about the farmyard. At the sight of the children, these came hurrying up, while from a dovecot at one end of the yard a cloud of white pigeons came fluttering down to join in the feast.

There were "Oohs!" and "Aahs!" of delight from the children as the birds scratched about around their feet and even took grains of wheat from their hands. One or two, Dawn especially, seemed nervous of some of the bigger birds, particularly a white gander that flapped his wings, stretched out his long neck, and hissed at them. Duncan, his appetite restored as well as his colour, chewed some of the corn thoughtfully before deciding he didn't much like the taste.

It did not occur to Sophie to be frightened of the gander. She plodded up and stood before him.

Putting her hands on her hips, she flapped her elbows, stretched out her short neck, and hissed back at him. Embarrassed, the gander let out a loud honk and hastily led his wives away.

The farmer's wife, standing near, said to Sophie's teacher, "Well, she's certainly not frightened of animals."

Sophie remembered something that Aunt Al had said to her long ago, when she had been a bit wary of earwigs, and she used the same words now.

"No good being scared of animals if you're going to be a farmer," she said.

"Oh, you are, are you?" said the farmer's wife. "It's hard work, you know."

"I don't mind," Sophie said.

"And you have to get up very early."

"I like that."

"And you have to be out in all winds and weathers."

"That doesn't worry me."

"It's messy too – mucking out all the animals."

"I like doing that," said Sophie. "I clean out my rabbit Beano every day and put it all on a special rabbit dung heap that I make. It's good for the garden, it helps its futility."

"Fertility," said Sophie's teacher behind her hand.

"Anyway," said Sophie, "I think manure smells lovely. Cow is nice, and so is pig, but horse is best of all."

"Well, you'll be all right then," said the farmer's wife, "because we've got cows and pigs and horses to show you and a lot of other animals too. You'll get all the smells you could want."

* * *

Sophie had a lovely morning. As well as ordinary breeds of farm animals, there were some rare ones too, and Sophie thought how nice these would look on her farm when she should get it.

As well as Blossom and April and May and Shorty and Measles, she felt she really must have a Longhorn cow because its horns were so long (and a Dexter cow because its legs were so short), and some Polish hens with feather hats on their heads, and a tiny miniature horse called a Falabella, and a Middle White pig with a squashed-in face.

"I'll just have to have a bigger farm," she said to Andrew.

At midday they ate their packed lunches in a huge old barn. All were hungry by now and they ate greedily, none more greedily than Duncan, who, despite having been sick on the coach, managed to get through the whole of his very full lunch-box.

After lunch the farmer himself appeared, leading a great big black Shire horse with huge hairy legs and feet like soup-plates, whose name was Henry VIII. Behind Henry VIII, trundling along over the cobblestones of the yard, was the most enormous four-wheeled wagon, painted red, white and blue, and called, so the farmer told them, the Ark Royal.

And everyone climbed aboard the Ark Royal, two by two, and off they all went for a tour of the farm. Sophie sat right at the front of the wagon, just behind Henry VIII's enormous bottom, and thought how beautiful and how strong he was, and how she simply must have one like him for her farm.

* * *

Only when they were almost back in the farmyard did it begin to rain, but then it tipped down, and everyone got off the Ark Royal and hurried down the yard towards the coach, which was by now waiting for them at the farm gate.

Safely inside, the teacher walked along the gangway, counting to make sure everyone was aboard.

She came to the place where Dawn and Duncan were seated on one side. On the other was Andrew, alone.

"Where's Sophie?" she asked him. Andrew jerked a thumb towards the window.

"Saying goodbye to Henry VIII," he said.

Looking out, the teacher could see the short stocky figure of Sophie, standing in the pouring rain, stroking the lowered velvety muzzle of the

great black horse. She went to the door of the
coach and called, "Sophie! Hurry up!"

"Please, miss," cried Dawn, "I don't want to sit
by Duncan. He might do it again."

"Oh, go and sit by Andrew, Duncan," said the
teacher, and again she called, "Come on, Sophie!
Quickly!"

If Sophie hadn't been hurrying, if the yard hadn't
been generously covered with the droppings of
chickens and ducks and geese and piglets, and if
the rain hadn't turned all that into a stinking slimy
soup, it might not have happened.

As it was, Sophie slipped and fell with a splash.

"Are you all right, Sophie?" asked the teacher
anxiously when at last the lady farmer arrived at
the coach.

"Bit dirty," said Sophie cheerfully, holding out

hands that were plastered with muck. Her clothes were covered in it, her face splashed with it.

"And a bit pongy," she added.

"Phew!" cried the other children as Sophie passed by on her way to her seat. But it was filled.

"Sit next to Dawn, Sophie," the teacher called.

Sophie looked at Dawn's horrified face and grinned.

"Don't mind if I do," she said.

Sophie
at the Concert

Sophie had a calendar on her bedroom wall. It bore a picture of an old-fashioned farming scene – thatched buildings, round haystacks, a duckpond and, between the shafts of a cart, a horse something like Henry VIII, led by a small boy in a smock-frock.

Under the picture was written:

To plough and sow,
To reap and mow,
And to be a farmer's boy.

Sophie had crossed out the last two words and written "lady farmer" instead. She also crossed out each day that passed as she waited anxiously for two very important dates, round each of which she had drawn a big red circle.

The first was of course Christmas Day – her birthday – and the second was New Year's Day, when she would start her riding lessons at Cloverlea Stables.

In the meantime the class's farming topic was finished, and everyone was preparing for the school's Christmas concert.

Last year Matthew and Mark had been

Tweedledum and Tweedledee in a production of bits of *Alice* (both *in Wonderland* and *Through the Looking-glass*). Sophie had been what she called "a crowd" in what she called an "activity play".

Unfortunately her father had told her what crowd players are supposed to say, so that while everyone in the Nativity play was quite silent when the Wise Men presented their gifts to the infant Jesus, Sophie shouted, "Rhubarb, rhubarb, rhubarb!"

This year the juniors were doing *The Wizard of Oz*, and the twins were Munchkins.

The infants were to do a play based on the story of *The Pied Piper of Hamelin*. There were plenty of parts in this for everyone – the Piper himself, the Mayor and Corporation, the townspeople, their children, and of course the rats.

Sophie was a rat.

She did not say anything
to her parents (because
she did not approve of
whingeing) but she was
secretly disappointed not to
have been given a bigger
part. Being a rat was no
better than being a
crowd – worse, in
fact, for all the rats
were allowed to do was squeak.

What she would really have liked to have been
was the Piper, dressed in a wonderful red and
yellow costume and playing "Come, follow, follow,
follow" at the head of, first, all the rats, and, later,
all the children.

Truth to tell, Sophie's teacher had considered her for the part, simply because Sophie was quite good at playing the recorder. But the Piper, the teacher knew, was meant to be male and tall and thin, none of which applied to Sophie, so she gave the part to a tall, thin recorder-playing boy called Justin.

But then, only two days before the concert, Fate took a hand as Justin took a tumble out of a tree and broke his arm. It was not a bad break, but all the same it isn't possible to play a recorder with one arm in plaster.

Hastily, Sophie's teacher held an audition of several other recorder players, including Sophie. Not only did Sophie play "Come, follow, follow, follow" just as well as Justin had, but it turned out that she, unlike the others, had learned the Piper's words as well.

"And she shouts them out good and loud," her teacher told the headmistress.

"Sophie may not be the world's best actor, but when she says, 'I will rid your town of rats,' you believe her. And when she stumps up to the Mayor and demands her thousand guilders for doing the job, you wonder how he dare refuse her."

At home, after the audition, Sophie said to the family, "You know our play."

"Yes," her mother said.

"*The Pied Piper of Hamelin*, isn't it?" her father said.

"Sophie's a rat!" sniggered the Munchkins.

Sophie resisted the temptation to call her brothers mowldy, stupid and assive.

Instead she said with dignity, "Actually, I am not a rat any more."

"Have you got the sack?" asked Mark.

"Did you forget your squeaks?" asked Matthew.

"No," said Sophie. "It's just that they needed an understeady."

"Understudy," said her mother. "For what?"

"Well, Justin's bust his arm so he can't do it, so they held an addition."

"Audition," said her father.

"For the Pied Piper, d'you mean?" asked Matthew.

"Yes," said Sophie.

"Who's going to do it then?" asked Mark.

"Me," said Sophie. "I am the Pied Piper of Hamelin."

They all stared at Sophie, short and stocky, her dark hair looking, as always, as though she had just come through a hedge backwards, and all of them

179

knew that, though small, she was very determined.

"If anyone can make a good job of it," her father said, "you will."

"I'm so pleased for you, darling," her mother said, and even the twins said, with one voice, "Good luck, Sophie."

"Thanks," said Sophie. "It'll be all right on the night."

And indeed it was.

The Wizard of Oz went very well, even though two of the Munchkins seemed rather more active and noisy than the rest.

But *The Pied Piper of Hamelin*, everyone agreed afterwards, was something else.

From the moment Sophie plodded on to the stage, in "queer long coat" (made for Justin, so much *too* long) "half of yellow and half of red"

and began to play,
there was no doubt
that all *would* follow
the small determined
Piper for the rest
of their lives.

Down off the stage,
and among the
audience, and all
around the school
hall plodded the
Pied Piper, while behind
her, first the rats scuttled and squeaked, and later,
the children of Hamelin skipped and danced.
And all the time Sophie played the tune of "Come,
follow, follow, follow" as loudly as she could, over
and over and over again. What's more, she hardly

made any mistakes, except once when she tripped over the skirts of that long coat, and then towards the end, when she ran out of puff.

How the audience cheered when it was over!

First, the Mayor (Andrew – a large cushion strapped to his tummy underneath his robes) came forward to the front of the stage and bowed, and then his Corporation, and then the townsfolk, and then their children (including one tall girl with fair hair done in bunches and tied with green ribbons), and then the rats (including one small fat boy rat who looked greedy enough to eat a whole cheese on his own).

But the loudest applause was reserved for the last to come forward, the Piper.

"Take your hat off and bow, Sophie," her teacher whispered, as she pushed her out from the wings.

And Sophie swept off her pointed cap, half red, half yellow, and bowed so low she nearly overbalanced.

That night Sophie went to bed very happy.

"I'm proud of you, Sophie," her teacher had said.

"Well done indeed, Sophie," the headmistress had said.

And when they got home, her mother and father had told her that she'd been the star of the show, and the ex-Munchkins had actually called her brilliant.

Sophie fell asleep still grinning.

When she woke next morning, she crossed off the previous day's date on the calendar. There were only a few left now until it would be Christmas and her birthday.

She got back into bed and addressed Tomboy, who was lying on her duvet as usual.

"Do you know, my dear," she said, "that I am going to be seven?"

"*Yeee-ooo?*" said the black cat in amazement, it seemed to Sophie.

"Yes, I am, and about time too. I've been six for years and years."

"*Neeee-o,*" said Tomboy.

"Well, one year anyway, but it seems like ages."

Sophie tickled the base of Tomboy's ears, making her purr like mad. Looking at her cat's sleek black coat made her think of Tomboy's son Ollie, who was also coal black, and thinking of Ollie made her think of Aunt Al, to whom Ollie belonged.

"Wouldn't it be nice," she said, "if only Aunt Al could be here to see me when I start my riding lessons? She's paying for them, after all. It's a pity she's so far away, stuck up on top of those old Highlands. I dare say she's sometimes lonely, with only a black cat for company."

"*Meee-ow?*" said Tomboy.

"No, not you, my dear. Your son Ollie," said Sophie.

She sighed.

"I wish Aunt Al could come to stay," she said, "but no such luck, I'm afraid."

Then she began to rub the tip of her nose.

"Tomboy," she said, "in case you didn't know, black cats are supposed to be lucky. But only if

they come to you from the right-hand side. Let's
see what you can do," and she lifted her cat up
and dropped her off the bed, on the right-hand
side of it.

Tomboy stretched herself, hooping her back and
scrabbling at the carpet, and then jumped straight
back up. For extra luck, Sophie crossed her fingers,
on both hands.

"I wish Aunt Al could come to stay," she said
again.

At breakfast, Sophie was eating Coco Pops, while
Puddle sat hopefully at her feet, waiting for her to
drop some.

Matthew and Mark had gobbled their food at top
speed as usual and disappeared.

Sophie's father was reading a newspaper.

Her mother was opening a letter.

She read it, and then said to her husband quietly, "It's from You-know-who."

"Oh," said Sophie's father from behind his paper. "Can she come?"

"Yes."

"For Christmas?"

"No. For Hogmanay, she says, and for a week after that."

Sophie swallowed a mouthful of Coco Pops.

"What's Hogmanay?" she asked.

"It's a special day for people in Scotland, the last day of the year."

I only know one person in Scotland, Sophie thought. She suddenly paused in the act of putting a loaded spoonful in her mouth. The spoon tilted a little and Puddle cleared up.

"Who's You-know-who?" she said.

Her father lowered his paper and looked at his wife and they smiled.

"Guess," they said.

"Aunt Al?" said Sophie softly.

"Yes."

"Coming to stay with us?"

"Yes. She arrives on the thirty-first of December."

"Yikes!" cried Sophie. "Tomboy did the trick!"

Sophie in the Dog-house

Christmas Day came and went. For Sophie it had the usual bonus – two presents from each person, one with "Happy Christmas" on it, one with "Many Happy Returns".

But Sophie had made sure that the other members of the family were not forgotten. She had raided her Farm Money and had bought what she thought were suitable gifts.

For her father – a large box of matches, to help him light that pipe of his that seemed always to be going out.

For her mother – a large bar of Lifebuoy soap. ("Not that you aren't quite clean, Mum," she said, "but this smells different from our usual stuff.")

For Matthew and Mark – sweets, as usual.

For Tomboy – a piece of coley from the fishmonger. ("Its real name is coalfish," he had told her. "Good," said Sophie. "Just right for a coal black cat.")

For Puddle – a big bone from the butcher.

For Beano – the biggest carrot in the greengrocer's.

For only one person had Sophie not bought anything, and that was the person who was going to give her the biggest, most expensive present ever, the course of riding lessons.

How could she compete with that? Whatever should she get Aunt Al? After Christmas she consulted her mother, who thought for a while and then said, "You know, rather than buying her something, I think that what Aunt Al would like best would be if you made her something, did it all by yourself, just for her, a special present."

"I can't make things," Sophie said. "I'm no good at that."

"I know!" her mother said. "Write her a poem. You did a lovely poem for your farming topic – your teacher showed me. Do one for Aunt Al."

"What about?"

"Well, it could be part of a Christmas card. You could draw a picture and write a poem too."

"But Christmas is over."

"Well, a New Year card then."

"OK," Sophie said. "I'll have a bash."

She did the picture first. After a lot of thought, she decided to draw a black cat. Cats weren't as hard to do as some things, and it was easy to colour it in with a black felt marker. Of course she drew it walking from right to left. Then she wrote OLLIE under it. The poem took longer, but Sophie worked away determinedly at it, occasionally asking questions like, "What rhymes with 'Scotland'?" or "What rhymes with 'the Highlands'?" or, "How old's Aunt Al going to be next year?"

At last she finished it, the day before Aunt Al was due to arrive. To Sophie's surprise, her father set off quite early on the morning of December the thirty-first to fetch his great-aunt from the railway station.

"The train's due in at nine a.m.," he said.

"Yikes!" cried Sophie. "You said she lived six hundred miles away. If she only started out this morning, it must be the fastest train in the world."

"No, no," her father said. "It's a ten-hour journey, but she has a sleeping compartment, you see. She'll have slept nearly all the way, I hope."

And indeed when Aunt Al did arrive, she looked as fresh as a daisy. Sophie waited till everyone else had gone off to do something or other, and then she produced her special present.

"I did this for you," she said. "It took an awful long time."

Aunt Al took the card in her skinny, bony old hands, curled like a bird's claws, and looked at the picture of the black cat, and read beneath it:

This is a poem for you Aunt Al
Because you are my speshial pal
And this year Mummy told me
You are going to be 83
So I wish you a Happy New Year
And I hope you will have a nice stay here
Where it is warmer than Scotland
Which is not a hot land
Speshially on top of the Highlands
The coldest place in the British Ilands
And the picture is of Ollie
And you can see his sister Dolly
Because she lives at Cloverlea
Riding Stables where I shall be
Going to ride on Saturday
And you are going to pay
So I am very pleased.
With love from your great great neece.

"It's a very good poem, Sophie," Aunt Al said.

"It is, isn't it," Sophie said.

"And it rhymes beautifully."

"It does, doesn't it."

"And it's the very nicest present you could have given me," said Aunt Al. "I shall treasure it. And talking of treasuring things, I brought something to show you."

She rummaged in her handbag and brought out an old snapshot.

"Have a look at that," she said.

Sophie took the photograph and studied it. It was not very clear and the picture was rather brownish, but she could see that it was of a small girl sitting on a pony.

"Who d'you think that is?" Aunt Al asked.

"Don't know," said Sophie. "Nobody I know."

"Turn it over then," said Aunt Al, so Sophie did, and written on the back in rather spidery and faded grown-up's writing was:

Alice on Frisk
Balnacraig 1920

"It's you!" Sophie said.

"Yes. I was nine."

"And was Frisk your pony?"

"Yes. He was rather a naughty pony but I loved him more than anything in the world."

"More than your mum and dad?"

"Well, no, perhaps not. But next best after them."

"I wish I could have a pony of my own," said Sophie.

"Wait till you're a lady farmer," said Aunt Al,

"and then have a horse, that's my advice. Now tell me – your first lesson is tomorrow, is that right?"

"Yes. It's not really the first. I did some riding in Cornwall."

"How much do you know about the tack?"

"Well," said Sophie, "there's a bridle and reins and a saddle. Oh, and a thing round the pony's tummy."

"The girth. What about a snaffle, what's that?"

"Don't know."

"It's a kind of bit, that goes in the horse's mouth, but it's jointed, so it isn't as harsh as a curb. And what's a numnah?"

"Don't know."

"It's a cloth or pad, a sheepskin sometimes, that goes under the saddle to stop it chafing."

"Gosh, you know a lot, Aunt Al," Sophie said.

"I was a good horsewoman once. Shall I tell you what I think will happen tomorrow?"

"Yes, please."

"Well, you'll all be riding your ponies inside an enclosed ring called a menage, and all round this ring there will be posts at intervals, each with a big letter on it. A K E H C M B F."

"Why?"

"So that the instructor can say to you, 'Right, now ride across from A to M,' or E to B, or whatever."

"Oh," said Sophie. "Do they always have those letters?"

"Yes," said Aunt Al, "and they always teach you the same way to remember them. 'All King Edward's Horses Can Manage Big Feeds.'"

"Oh," said Sophie. "I thought King Edward was a potato."

"Oh, Sophie," said Aunt Al. "You're going to be a farmer and no mistake."

Sophie woke on the Saturday morning and looked at the red circle round January the first.

"Happy New Year, my dear," she said to Tomboy, but the black cat only yawned.

Sophie looked at her watch. Seven o'clock. Only three hours to wait now. She got dressed and went downstairs to let Puddle out into the garden and to go to the potting-shed to feed Beano. Again she wished both animals a Happy New Year, but Puddle only barked at her because he wanted her to throw a stick, and Beano only wiffled his nose at her because he never said anything anyway.

At breakfast, though, everyone else returned her good wishes.

"This year," said Sophie's mother to Aunt Al, "Sophie will become a junior."

"Fancy!" said Aunt Al. "Do you look forward to that, Sophie?"

"Yes," said Sophie. "Then I can do judo and throw Dawn down on the mat."

"Who's Dawn?" asked Aunt Al.

"A girl in Sophie's class," said Mark.

"Sophie can't stand her," said Matthew.

"Why not?"

"She's a wimp," said Sophie.

She looked at her watch.

"Only an hour and a half to go," she said. "We ought to be getting ready."

"It's only a ten-minute drive to Cloverlea Stables," her mother said. "By the way, who's coming to watch Sophie's riding lesson?"

"I'm playing golf,"
said Sophie's father.

"We're playing football,"
said the twins.

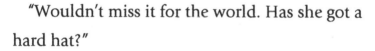

"Aunt Al?"

"Wouldn't miss it for the world. Has she got a
hard hat?"

"No," said Sophie's mother. "They supply them
with a proper jockey skull cap with a silk over it."

"What about jodhpurs?"

"Jeans will have to do. I dare say some of the
others will have fancy clothes but Sophie doesn't
mind, do you, darling?"

"No," said Sophie. "All you need is a good seat."

"Attagirl!" said Aunt Al.

It was a good job that Sophie wasn't fussy,
because when they arrived the three other little

girls already there were rather smartly dressed. Meg
Morris greeted them, and everyone was introduced,
including Dolly, who came running up to rub
against Sophie.

"We're just waiting for the last of the group,"
said Meg, and then, "Oh, here she comes now," as
another car drew up.

Out of it stepped first Dawn's mother and then
Dawn.

"Yuk!" said Sophie loudly.

Dawn was kitted out in skin-tight breeches,
polished riding boots, a natty checked hacking
jacket, and under it a silk blouse topped by a stock
with a gold pin through it. She was even wearing
a little bowler hat. She looked a perfect fashion
plate. She also looked nervous, until she caught
sight of Sophie, when she looked *very* nervous.

Dawn's mother also looked uncomfortable when she recognized Sophie's mother, and they nodded awkwardly at one another as Meg Morris took the five little girls away to introduce them to their ponies.

"Aunt Al," said Sophie's mother. "D'you mind if I just nip off to do some shopping? I shan't be long. I'll be back to see Sophie performing. Will you be all right?"

"Of course," said Aunt Al.

She watched as the five children returned, each leading her pony, and as Meg showed them in turn how to tighten their girths, pull down their stirrups, and then how to mount.

Four of them seemed quite at home in the saddle, but gawky Dawn sat awkwardly, shooting anxious glances towards her mother.

"Now then," said Meg Morris, "I'm going to walk

right round with each of you in turn. We'll go on the left rein – that's anticlockwise – from this post marked A, right round to the post marked F."

"All King Edward's Horses Can Manage Big Feeds," said Sophie.

"Well done, Sophie!" said Meg. "Fancy knowing that!"

Sophie looked pleased.

Three of the other girls looked puzzled.

Dawn looked pale.

As Meg Morris moved off around the menage with the first of the children, Aunt Al came forward to the rails to stand beside Sophie's pony.

"Sophie," she said in a low voice. "That girl behind you. D'you know her?"

"Not half," said Sophie. "That's Dawn, that is."

"She's nervous," said Aunt Al.

"Of course she is," said
Sophie. "She's a wimp," and she looked round
scornfully at Dawn.

"We can't all be brave, you know," said Aunt Al.
"Why don't you say something nice to her, to
encourage her?"

"You must be joking," said Sophie rudely.

"I am not joking, Sophie," said Aunt Al, and
there was a steely edge to her voice. "If you cannot

do a simple kindness, then though this is your first lesson, it may well be your last. I am not paying out good money for bad behaviour," and she turned away and walked off on her thin bird's legs.

Sophie went very red in the face.

Then she turned in her saddle to face Dawn, who looked, if possible, even more unhappy at this.

"What's the matter with you?" said Sophie gruffly.

"I don't like it," said Dawn miserably. "I might fall off."

Sophie looked at Dawn's long legs.

"Well, it isn't far if you do," she said.

"I'm frightened," said Dawn.

Sophie took a deep breath.

"Look, Dawn," she said in as kindly a voice as she could manage, "you'll be all right. There's

nothing to be scared of. All you've got to do is
sit there and the lady will hold on to your bridle.
You can't come to any harm, honestly. And if you
don't like it, well, then you needn't come back
here any more."

And I hope you don't, she thought.

So amazed was Dawn to be spoken to by Sophie
in such an almost friendly way that she quite forgot
her fears and allowed herself to be led around
in a daze.

Her mother watched, smiling.

Aunt Al watched, poker-faced.

Sophie's mother returned from her shopping in
time to see her daughter being told to "Walk on".

It did not take Meg Morris long to realize that
Sophie, for all her lack of experience, was a natural
rider, and she treated her differently from the

others, who watched admiringly, especially the now pink-cheeked Dawn. Soon she had Sophie changing rein, to go clockwise around the menage, and then it was "Trot on", with Sophie rising in her saddle to the manner born.

When the lesson was over, and Sophie plodded up to join them, her mother said, "Well done, darling, you rode very well."

Aunt Al said, "Well done, Sophie. Now you can look forward to the rest of your riding lessons."

She looked directly down at Sophie with her sharp blue eyes, and Sophie knew exactly what she meant, and they grinned at one another.

"She does ride well, doesn't she?" said Sophie's mother.

"Not bad," said Aunt Al. "Just needs a touch of the whip now and then."

Sophie
at the Farm

Aunt Al's visit ended before Sophie's second riding lesson. They parted the best of friends.

"I shall have your poem framed and hang it on my bedroom wall, Sophie," Aunt Al said. "And mind and let me know how the rest of the lessons go. I think you'll make a fine horsewoman."

"Horsegirl," Sophie said.

"Yes, but time flies, and you'll be a woman before you can say 'Jack Robinson'."

"Jack Robinson!" said Sophie quickly, grinning.

"And when you're a bit older, you must come and visit me and Ollie. You'd love the Highlands."

"Just me, alone?" said Sophie.

"Well, it would be nice if all the family could come, this summer perhaps – your father talks about having a Scottish holiday one year – but yes, I should like it very much if you came by yourself, once you're old enough to make the journey on your own. Say in about – let's see – eight years' time, when you'll be fifteen."

Sophie did a sum in her head.

"But you'll be ninety then," she said, "if…" and she stopped.

"If I haven't kicked the bucket, you were going to say," said Aunt Al. "Don't worry, Sophie, I have every intention of scoring a century and getting

that telegram from the Queen. My father lived
to be a hundred and two and three-quarters,
so I've got form."

"Will Ollie still be alive?" Sophie asked.

"Don't see why not. He's still got
all nine lives left."

When it came to the actual time to
say goodbye, Sophie supposed they
would shake hands, as they always
had done before. Neither of them
were great kissers. But as it was, she
found herself flinging her arms
round Aunt Al's skinny middle
and burying her face against her,
while her great-great-aunt stroked her tousled mop
of dark hair. And as Aunt Al was driven away to the

railway station while they all waved goodbye, Sophie
shouted, "See you!" and Aunt Al called back, "Sure
thing!" and then she was gone.

The following day Sophie went to Cloverlea Stables
for her second lesson. To her relief, she found that
Dawn had not turned up. She had not wanted to
go on being nice to her, and now she needn't.

"Is Dawn ill?" she said to Meg Morris.

"No," said Meg. "She's not coming any more."

"Oh dear," said Sophie. "What a shame."

"I think perhaps she's not the horsy type," said
Meg.

"No," said Sophie. "She wants to be a hairdresser."

She knew this because last term her class had
had to write down what they would like to be
when they grew up.

A lot of boys wanted to be professional footballers or racing drivers, and nursing or teaching were popular choices for the girls, though there were several, including Dawn, who chose hairdressing. Andrew of course wrote "Farmer" and Sophie "Lady Farmer". Duncan wrote "Cook", and when asked why, said simply, "I like food".

At the start of the new term, Sophie tackled her father on the subject of pocket money. Due to the cost of the Christmas presents she had bought, her Farm Money was now down to nine pounds, ten pence.

"I've been collecting for three years," she said to her father, "so I'm only making about three pounds a year. What d'you call someone who is really poor?"

"A pauper?" said her father.

"Well," said Sophie, "I'm pauper than anyone else."

She had worked out a sum on a piece of paper and now she produced it.

"Look," she said. "I want to have enough money to buy a farm by the time I'm grown up, which is eighteen these days, which is in eleven years and three times eleven is thirty-three, plus what I've got now makes forty-two pounds, ten. How am I going to become a lady farmer if I've only got forty-two pounds?"

"Perhaps you'll marry a farmer," her father said. "That's one way to do it."

"I am not marrying Andrew unless he gets his father's farm," said Sophie.

"When the father retires, you mean?"

"Or dies," said Sophie matter-of-factly. "He's quite old."

I shouldn't think he's forty yet, thought Sophie's father. About my age in fact.

"Well, you'll just have to save harder, Sophie," he said.

"I ought to be on Family Insistence," Sophie said.

"Assistance, you mean?"

"You can call it what you like," said Sophie. "I mean, more pocket money. I'm seven now. I ought to have one pound a week, like Matthew and Mark do. It's not fair. I get 50p and they get two pounds."

"But there are two of them."

"It's all because I'm a girl," said Sophie. "Women ought to be paid the same as men."

Sophie's father felt himself wilting before his daughter's determination.

"Oh, very well then," he said. "I'll put your pocket money up to one pound a week."

"Thanks, Daddy," said Sophie.

She consulted her piece of paper again.

"It's more than two weeks since my birthday," she said, "so now you owe me two extra 50ps already."

"Oh, Sophie," said her father. "You're going to be a businesswoman and no mistake. Andrew could do worse. He'll be a lucky chap if he decides to marry you."

Sophie rubbed the tip of her nose.

"He won't decide," she said, "but you've given me an idea."

In the playground next day Sophie said to Andrew, "I haven't been to tea with you yet this term."

"It's only the second day," said Andrew.

"I still haven't been. You'd better get your mum to ask me."

"Oh, all right."

So a couple of days after that, Andrew's mother asked Sophie's mother if Sophie could come to tea.

"I'll try to keep her from falling in cowpats or into the duckpond," she said.

Before tea Andrew's father took both children to have a look at a sow that had had a litter of ten piglets only the night before. As they looked through the bars of the pen in which the sow lay nursing her already fat pink babies, Sophie said to Andrew's father, "How old are you?"

"I'll be forty this year," he said.

"When are you going to retire?"

Andrew's father smiled.

"Not yet awhile, Sophie," he said. "In another twenty years perhaps, when Andrew's old enough to takeover."

"Oh," said Sophie. "He's going to, is he?"

"I hope so. This farm's been handed down from father to son for a long time now."

"I shall drive all the tractors," Andrew said.

"He's clever with his hands," said his father. "Makes some wonderful models with Lego. Should be good with the mechanical side of things."

"I'm good with animals," said Sophie. "I'm going to be a lady farmer, you know."

Andrew's father looked at the two seven-year-olds, one very fair, almost white-haired, one dark, standing side by side at the pig pen. Just suppose … in twenty years' time … he said to himself. Andrew could do worse.

After tea Andrew and Sophie were watching children's TV. At least, Andrew was watching. Sophie was thinking. Presently she said, "How much pocket money do you get?"

"One pound a week," said Andrew.

Sophie nodded. I was right, she thought.

"And how much money have you got saved?" she said.

"About two hundred pounds," said Andrew.

"Don't be silly, Andrew," said Sophie. "How much really?"

"I got twenty pounds altogether for Christmas that I haven't spent yet."

"You don't want to go spending it," Sophie said. "You want to save it."

"Oh, all right," said Andrew, who wanted to watch the programme uninterrupted.

"You ought to be able to save 50p a week," said Sophie.

"Oh, all right."

"And if I can do the same, well, in twenty years'

time we'll have a nice lot between us. And then I shan't have to buy a farm and the animals will all be here already and your dad can have a nice rest and you'll be the farmer and I'll be the lady farmer."

Andrew, glued to the screen, did not answer.

Sophie sighed.

"Andrew," she said, "listen to me."

"What?"

"When we're grown up, I'm going to marry you."

"Oh, all right."

That evening, when Sophie's parents came to her bedroom to say goodnight, she was looking, they thought, particularly happy. Tomboy, lying on her feet, was purring loudly.

"What's up with you?" her mother said. "You look like the cat that's eaten the cream."

"They look like two cats," her father said, "that have eaten two lots of cream."

"Well," said Sophie, "I've something to tell you. I'll write to Aunt Al and tell her, but don't say anything to the boys, they wouldn't understand."

"Understand what?" they said. "What is it you've got to tell us?"

Sophie sat up in bed.

"I wanted you to be the first to know," she said. "I'm engaged."

Sophie's
Lucky

Contents

In Which Sophie Makes a Phone Call

"What a pity, my dear," said Sophie, "that you had to have that operation."

She was lying in bed, stroking the furry stomach of her black cat Tomboy, who replied with a contented purr.

A couple of years earlier Tomboy had given birth

to four kittens, and that, Sophie's parents had decided, was enough.

So, despite Sophie's protests, Tomboy had been taken to the vet and spayed. Thinking again about this as she stroked her cat, Sophie remembered how angry she had been.

"They were mowldy, stupid and assive, they were," she said, "doing that to you. You'd have liked loads more babies, wouldn't you?"

For answer, the black cat made a noise that sounded like *"Neee-o!"*

* * *

Sophie looked at the four pictures on her bedroom walls – of a cow, two hens, a pig and a Shetland pony.

"Nobody's going to do operations on you, my dears," she said, "I can tell you. Blossom, you're going to have lots of calves, and April and May will have masses of chicks, and Measles will have loads of piglets, and Shorty – oh no, I forgot, you're a boy, Shorty, so you can't be a mother."

Thinking about the pony led Sophie to remembering the course of riding lessons she had recently had, lessons paid for by her great, great friend, her great-great-aunt, known to all the family simply as Aunt Al.

Sophie sat up in bed with a jerk, dislodging Tomboy, who stalked out of the room, tail waving angrily.

"Aunt Al doesn't know!" she said.

She rubbed the tip of her nose, a sign of deep thought.

"I know! I'll ring her up. I must tell her that I'm engaged," she said.

Sophie's best friend at school was Andrew, a stocky, fair-haired little boy to whom Sophie had recently proposed marriage.

Since her ambition had always been to become a lady farmer when grown up, and since Andrew's father had a farm, marriage – in due course – seemed to Sophie the obvious solution.

Andrew, busy watching television on the occasion of the proposal, had simply replied, "Oh, all right" to everything that Sophie had said, and so was unaware of his fate.

Sophie got dressed and went downstairs.

Her twin brothers, Matthew and Mark, had already started their breakfasts. They were nine (though Matthew was ten minutes older than Mark), and life for them was a sort of race. Everything they did had to be done, it seemed, at speed, in competition with one another, and it was plain to Sophie that each was set on eating up his cornflakes before the other.

As they finished (a dead-heat), the toaster popped

identical twin slices and they leaped to their feet and ran for them.

Sophie waited until her brothers had finished eating their toast (Matthew lost this race by a short crust)

and gone out of the room, and then she said,
"Mum, can I ring up Aunt Al?"

"Whatever for?"

"To tell her."

"Tell her what?"

Sophie sighed. She raised her left hand and
pointed to its third finger.

"About me and Andrew, of course."

Her mother smiled.

"Wanted to wait till the boys had gone, did you?"

Sophie nodded.

"They wouldn't understand," she said. "They're too
inmature."

Her mother smiled.

Her father said, "Anyway, the answer is no. You
are not making a long distance phone call to the
Highlands of Scotland at this time of the morning

– it's too expensive, and anyway, the old lady will probably still be in bed."

Sophie's face darkened.

"She will not," she said. "She always gets up early to give Ollie his breakfast."

Ollie was a son of Tomboy, black like his mother. Sophie had given him to Aunt Al, who in return had given her great-great-niece a white rabbit with pink eyes and a wiffly nose called Beano.

"I shall just have to pay for the call myself then," said Sophie. "I'll have to use this week's pocket money for it."

Sophie's mother and father looked at their daughter, wearing as usual old jeans and a very old blue jersey (now much too small for her) with "Sophie" in white letters still dimly visible on it. They saw, under the shock of dark hair, the set expression on her face.

Then they looked at one another.

Sophie, they both knew, though small, was very determined, and it was unlikely, they both knew, that they would win this particular battle.

"This evening perhaps?" said Sophie's mother to her husband. "It's cheaper then."

"Oh, I suppose so," said Sophie's father. "And you don't have to use your precious pocket money, Sophie."

"Thanks, Mum. Thanks, Daddy," Sophie said.

Sophie did not approve of a lot of kissing or suchlike displays of affection, but she got up from the table, and patted her mother and rubbed the top of her head against her father's arm.

"It won't be an expensive phone call," she said. "Aunt Al's like me, she doesn't like a long conservation."

"Don't you mean conversation?" they said.

"Oh, she's all in favour of that," said Sophie. "You know, saving the rainy forests and stopping animals from becoming distinct."

Sophie spent quite some time that day thinking about Aunt Al, perched up there on the Highlands, surrounded by red deer and golden eagles and blue hares. She lived, Sophie knew, in a big, rambling old house called Balnacraig.

"I was born there," Aunt Al had told her once, "in 1911, and I've been there ever since. My brothers and sisters grew up and married and went away, but I stayed on to look after my mother and father. When they died, Balnacraig was left to me."

I wish I could see Aunt Al's house, Sophie thought now. I wish we could go to the Highlands one day, climb right up on the top, I mean.

"You'd like that, Puddle, wouldn't you?" she said to her dog, a small white terrier with a black patch over his right eye, and he wagged his tail in agreement. Strictly speaking, Puddle didn't belong to Sophie in the way that Tomboy and Beano did; he was the family's dog. But Sophie considered him to be hers, and he much preferred her company to anyone else's.

That evening, Sophie made sure that Matthew and Mark were busy elsewhere, and then she dialled Aunt Al's number.

As usual, she was amazed to hear that familiar
voice come rushing down the steep slopes of
those very high Highlands and along all those
hundreds of miles of telephone wires, all in the
blink of an eye.

"Hello, Aunt Al," she said. "It's me."

"Sophie!" said Aunt Al. "What a nice surprise!"

"Yes," said Sophie. "I've got another one for
you too. It's about my friend Andrew."

"The farmer's son?"

"Yes. We're engaged to be married. I thought you'd
like to know."

"Congratulations," said Aunt Al. "That's
good news. By the way, how's your Farm Money
going?"

For three years now Sophie had been saving up
towards her ambition, and had recently persuaded

her father to increase her pocket money to one pound per week.

"It was down to nine pounds and ten pence," Sophie said, "but now it's up to eleven pounds and ten pence. And I've told Andrew he's got to save fifty pence a week. By the way, how's Ollie?"

"Very well," said Aunt Al. "Would you like to see him again?"

"Oh yes," said Sophie, "but how?"

"I mentioned to your father, last time I stayed with you, that perhaps you'd all like a Scottish holiday this summer. How about coming to stay with me for a couple of weeks, what do you say to that?" said Aunt Al, and then she hastily held the receiver away from her ear as back up the hundreds of miles of wire came a loud shout of "Yikes!"

In Which Sophie Goes Out to Tea

In the playground at school, Sophie said to Andrew, "Have you ever been to Scotland?"

"Can't remember," Andrew said.

Sophie knew that this meant he hadn't but wasn't going to admit it.

"We're going there in the summer holidays," she said.

"To stay on a farm?" asked Andrew. Last summer Sophie had, he knew, stayed on a farm in Cornwall.

"No. With my Aunt Al. On top of the Highlands."

"Sheep," said Andrew in a knowledgeable voice. "You'll see lots of sheep. Scotch Blackfaces."

Some boys rushed by, kicking a football, and Andrew dashed to join in. Sophie looked about for someone else who might be interested in her news, and her eye fell upon Dawn.

Dawn, tall for her age, with golden hair done in bunches, and dark, stocky Sophie were as different as chalk and cheese. Normally Sophie would never have bothered to speak to Dawn, but now she did, remembering something that had happened recently at Cloverlea Stables. Sophie had called Dawn a wimp for being nervous of horses, and Aunt Al had told Sophie off very sharply for being unkind.

So I'll be kind now, thought Sophie, and speak to the wimp.

"Dawn!" she called.

Dawn approached, as twitchily as though Sophie was a wild bronco.

"What is it?" she said.

"Have you ever been to Scotland?" Sophie said.

"I've been to Cornwall," Dawn said nervously.

"I know that," growled Sophie (for Sophie and Dawn had met on a Cornish beach and it had not been a happy meeting), "but have you ever been to Scotland?"

"No," said Dawn.

"I'm going there, in the summer holidays."

"Oh," said Dawn.

At that point Duncan appeared.

Duncan was a small, fat ginger-haired boy,

whom Sophie had once considered as a possible worker on her farm in due course, but he'd got the sack before he'd begun. He was a very greedy little boy and he trailed about after Dawn, whose parents gave her lots of sweets.

"What about you, Duncan?" said Sophie. "Have you ever been to Scotland?"

"Course I have," said Duncan. "I'm Scottish. Can I have a sweet, Dawn?"

"He wears a kilt," said Dawn.

"Yuk!" said Sophie. "How d'you know he does, anyway?"

"He was wearing one when he came to my party."

"What party?"

"My birthday party."

"You didn't invite me," said Sophie.

"No," said Dawn.

"Give us a sweet," said Duncan.

Dawn gave him one, and he waddled away, chewing.

Fancy him in a kilt, thought Sophie, it'd be like a miniskirt. Anyway, I wouldn't have gone to her rotten party if she'd asked me. Just wait till we're juniors and we can start doing judo. She imagined Dawn crashing down on the mat.

"In September," she said, "I'll be doing judo, Dawn."

Dawn looked at Sophie and knew what she was thinking. Wide-eyed, slightly buck-toothed, and with her bunches drooping down like lop ears, Dawn resembled a long, thin rabbit staring helplessly at a fierce and thickset stoat.

"You'll be doing judo too, won't you?" said

the stoat, and feebly the hypnotised rabbit
answered, "Yes," but thought, *No, no!*

When school ended that day, Sophie's mother
and Andrew's mother were chatting away as they
waited for their children.

"I expect you know," Sophie's mother said,
"that my daughter and your son are engaged to
be married?"

Andrew's mother laughed.

"Are they?" she said. "He actually asked her to
marry him, did he?"

"I doubt it," said Sophie's mother. "More likely
she told him he was going to. Here they come now."

"You haven't asked me to tea yet this term,"
Sophie was saying to Andrew.

"Well, it's only just started."

"Well, you haven't asked me."

"Why don't you ask me?" said Andrew. "Why do you always have to come to tea at our house?"

"Because you live on a farm, of course, silly," said Sophie, "and something's always having babies. Go on, ask your mum to ask me."

"Mum," said Andrew when he reached her, "can Sophie come to tea?"

"Today?"

Andrew turned to Sophie.

"Today?" he said.

Sophie nodded.

"Thanks," she said.

"Are you sure?" said Sophie's mother.

Andrew's mother nodded, smiling.

"Of course," she said, and to Sophie, "One of our best cows had a lovely pair of twins yesterday. Bull calves, unfortunately."

"Twin boys," said Sophie, shaking her head.
"They're not much use. I should know."

When Andrew's father came in for his tea before
starting the evening milking, Sophie said to him,
"Have you ever been to Scotland?"

"Why, yes, Sophie, years ago," he said.

"To the Highlands?"

"Yes. Wonderful country – mountains and glens
and lochs. I remember once sitting by the side of
Loch Ness, and what d'you think I saw?"

"The Monster!" Sophie said.

Andrew's father – a keen bird-watcher – smiled.

"No," he said. "I saw a Slavonian Grebe, a
beautiful little diver with a black head striped with
gold. I wish I had seen the Monster, mind you."

"Is there one, Dad?" said Andrew.

"The local people believe there are lots. Loch Ness is a huge stretch of water, you know, twenty-four miles long and as deep as three hundred metres in places. Plenty of room in those depths for a creature like that."

"Like what?" said Sophie.

"Probably a plesiosaurus."

"Yikes!" said Sophie. "I hope I see one."

"Are you going to Scotland then, Sophie?" said Andrew's mother.

"Yes. In the summer holidays."

"And when they're over, you and Andrew won't be Infants any more, you'll be Juniors."

"Yes, and I'll be doing judo," said Sophie, "but they still don't give you Farming Lessons, I asked Matthew and Mark. You're lucky, you are, Andrew. I wish I lived on a farm."

"Perhaps one day
you'll marry a farmer,
Sophie," said
Andrew's mother.

Sophie nodded.

"I shall," she said.
"Can I have some
more cake?"

The farmer and
his wife looked
at the two heads,
one dark, one fair,

almost white, each bent over a plate of cake, and
then they looked at one another and smiled.

At home that evening, when her own father came
up to her room to say goodnight, Sophie said to

him, "Whereabouts in Scotland is Balnacraig, Daddy?"

"It's near Drumochter Pass, in the Grampian Mountains."

"How far from Loch Ness?"

"Oh, I suppose about twenty miles as the eagle flies. Probably a hundred by road."

"Can we go there when we're staying with Aunt Al?"

"Think we might see the Monster, eh?"

"Yes, and they very much want us to see them, they must do."

"Why?"

"Well," said Sophie, "Andrew's father told us. The animal is called Please-you-saw-us."

In Which
Sophie Is
Bowled Over

Sophie of course told both Tomboy and Puddle about the coming trip to Scotland. Tomboy, she felt sure, would be interested because of Ollie.

"I'll give him your love, my dear, never fear," said Sophie.

Puddle was to be taken with them. Sophie had been at her most determined about this.

"If he doesn't go, then I don't go," she said to her parents. "You'll have to put me in kennels too."

She had tried to interest Beano in the news (he had, after all, been a gift from Aunt Al), but the big white rabbit just gazed blankly at her with his pink eyes. Not for one moment would Sophie have allowed that Beano was stupid, but conversation with him tended to be one-sided.

Tomboy usually purred or mewed in reply to what she had to say, and Puddle wagged, or indeed barked, if she used an excited tone of voice. But Beano just wiffled his nose.

To make up for his silence, Sophie always talked to him a great deal.

One Saturday afternoon she spent a long time in the potting-shed, giving Beano's hutch a specially thorough clean, and chattering busily

away to him as he pottered about the floor.

When all was ready – his water-bottle and his hay-rack filled, his rabbit-mixture in his feeding-bowl with a nice carrot beside it, the hutch floor carpeted with fresh sawdust – Sophie stood, hands on hips, regarding her rabbit with the critical eye of a would-be lady farmer.

"You, my dear," she said, "are looking too fat. You haven't had enough exercise lately."

When Beano had first arrived, Sophie had tried exercising him on a lead. She had bought, out of her Farm Money, a smart blue collar and lead, originally for Tomboy (who didn't care for this), and in summertime she would drop the loop of the lead over a stake

driven into the lawn, and Beano would graze happily round it in a circle. On the arrival of Puddle, Sophie had sold the collar and lead back to the family (for Puddle was the family's dog, not hers alone) for a profit.

"We'll borrow them back," said Sophie now to Beano. "Puddle won't mind lending them. And then I'm going to take you for a nice long walk in the garden, before it gets too dark."

In fact, taking Beano for a walk meant being taken for a walk by Beano, who was only interested in going his own way. The big rabbit was strong, and he towed Sophie about the garden, to the amusement of Matthew and Mark, who were still, in the fading light, playing one-a-side football on the lawn: two bamboo poles were stuck in the grass at either end, as goals.

Suddenly, Beano took it into his head to try to run across the pitch, while Sophie hauled on his lead to no avail.

At the same time one of the boys took a shot at goal, and the ball struck Sophie full on the side of her head. Dazed, she fell to her knees, letting go of the lead. "Gosh, sorry, Sophie!" the kicker cried, and "He didn't mean to!" cried his opponent, and they both squatted anxiously beside their sister.

"Don't cry," they said.

"I'm not," said Sophie.

Sophie did not approve of crying.

"Are you all right?" they said.

Sophie shook her head.

"I feel a bit dizzy," she said.

"You better come inside," said Mark.

"And sit down for a bit," said Matthew, and they each took one of Sophie's arms and raised her up and marched her off the pitch.

"Mum!" they shouted. "Sophie's injured!"

Then they explained what had happened, and Mark said that it was he who had kicked the ball, and Matthew said that Mark hadn't meant to hurt Sophie, and Sophie said she had a bit of a headache, and their mother said that Sophie had better lie down on the sofa for a bit.

Which she did.

But after a while she suddenly remembered – Beano! She'd dropped the lead when the ball hit her. Beano was still out, in the dark garden.

"Quick!" she shouted, leaping to her feet. "We must find him!"

"Find who?" they all said.

"My rabbit. He's loose in the garden!" cried Sophie, and she rushed out.

"Go with her, boys," their mother said, "while I make sure the gate into the road is shut, and then I'll come and help you look."

By now it was quite dark, and though they all searched for ages with a torch – over the lawn, in the flower-beds, in the vegetable patch and through the shrubbery – there was no sign of Beano.

"Perhaps he's hopped back into the potting-shed," said Sophie's mother. But he hadn't. There in the torchlight was his hutch, beautifully clean but quite empty. He had simply disappeared.

"The gate was shut, wasn't it, Mum?" said Sophie.

"Yes."

"He must be somewhere in the garden," Sophie said.

"Of course he is. We'll find him, don't worry. Let's all go and have some tea now – it's getting rather cold out here – and then we'll have another search and I expect he'll have come out from wherever he's hiding."

Sophie would not eat any tea.

"I couldn't," she said. "Not when Beano hasn't had his."

Afterwards all five of them – for the children's father had returned from the golf club – put on coats (it was beginning to freeze) and mounted another search, but in vain.

At last they gave up – at least, four of them did. Sophie plodded doggedly on, prepared to go on all night if needs be. But, for once, her parents proved more determined than she was and insisted that she go to bed.

"There's nothing more we can do tonight," they said. "You snuggle down and go to sleep now, there's a good girl."

"I couldn't," Sophie said. "Not while Beano's out in the cold."

For a long time she didn't, but then at last, tired out, she fell deeply asleep.

Sophie woke early the following morning with

the feeling that something was terribly wrong, and
then she remembered and jumped out of bed and
ran to the window.

It was just growing light, and the lawn, she could
see, was white with frost. But on it there was no
large white lolloping shape. Nothing stirred in the
garden below, except – what was that?

Something was moving, along the top of the
garden wall, some animal, the size of a small dog
or a large cat. It walked along
the wall and then stopped
and sat there, looking down
towards the potting-shed. It
was reddish in colour, Sophie
could see now as the light grew
stronger, with a sharp pointed
face and a bushy tail.

It was a fox!

Before Sophie could think what to do, another animal appeared, a white one. Out from beneath the potting-shed, under which he had burrowed last evening to spend a comfortable night, emerged Beano. He hopped out on to the lawn, the blue collar around his neck, the blue lead trailing behind him, and sniffed curiously at the frosted grass. Each hop took him nearer to the watching fox.

"Look out, Beano, look out!" yelled Sophie at the top of her voice, but the double-glazing of her window deadened the sound, as the fox slipped down from the wall top, eyes fixed upon the approaching rabbit.

At that instant a third animal appeared upon the scene: a black animal, an angry animal, furious at the sight and the rank smell of this

red bushy-tailed intruder into her garden.

Tomboy's ears were flat upon her head, her back arched, her coat stood on end, and suddenly she launched herself, spitting and yowling, straight at the fox, which turned tail and leaped back over the wall and was gone.

Matthew and Mark had slept through Sophie's loud shout, but it had woken her mother and father from their Sunday morning lie-in, and now they looked from their window to see Sophie, in dressing-gown and slippers, being towed by Beano back to the potting-shed and his nice clean hutch and his supper-become-breakfast.

Behind them, her tail raised high in triumph, her coat very black against the frosty grass, stalked Sophie's victorious Tomboy.

In Which Sophie Dreams a Dream

At breakfast Sophie said to the others, "Yikes! You should have seen it! Tomboy was as fierce as a tiger! He was intimated, that old fox was."

"You mean he was intimidated," her father said.

"I mean he was absolutely putrified."

"Petrified," said her mother.

"Call it what you like," said Sophie. "He was scared stiff."

The twins paused in the middle of their cornflake race for Matthew to say, "Good old Tomboy," and Mark to say, "Lucky old Beano," before they went on shovelling the stuff in.

"Fancy your cat saving your rabbit's life," said Sophie's mother, and her father said, "You ought to reward her. Give her something nice to eat. What does she like best?"

"Fish," Sophie said. "She likes fish."

"What sort?"

Matthew swallowed hastily, winning the race by a short flake, and said, "I know!"

Mark swallowed too and said, "I know what you're going to say!" and together they chanted, "Pilchards in tomato sauce!"

"Yuk!" said Sophie. They were her least favourite food.

"Don't be so mowldy, stupid and assive," she
went on, automatically but not in anger. "Pilchards
in tomato sauce are indelible."

"Indelible?" said her mother.

"Inedible," said her father.

"Mummy," said Sophie. "Got any fish fingers?"

"There's a packet in the freezer. You can have one
for Tomboy if you like."

"Only one?" said Sophie. "That's mean."

"All right, two then."

Later, in the potting-shed, Sophie said, "I'm
sorry, my dear, this is all they'd let me have."

She stroked Tomboy, and went on, "I put them
under the cushion in Dad's chair when he wasn't
looking, and he's been sitting on them all the time
he was reading the Sunday papers, so they should
have unfrozen nicely."

She sat watching her cat eating, and then she let Beano out of his hutch, and put on the collar and lead once more. The boys, she knew, had gone to play with friends, so there would be no danger from flying footballs.

"And don't worry about that old fox," she said to her rabbit. "He won't come back in a hurry."

The sun was shining, the frost was gone, and there was a feeling in the air that spring was only just around the corner.

Beano must have felt this, for he buck-jumped about in a very bouncy way, while Puddle barked approvingly, and Tomboy lay in a patch of sunshine and licked the last of the fish fingers from her lips.

After a while Sophie tied Beano's lead to the leg of a garden seat and sat down, while Puddle jumped up beside her.

She looked in turn at her three animals and thought how lucky she was to have them.

"But I must tell you, my dear," she said to Puddle, rubbing the roots of his ears – something he specially liked – "that there is another animal I would very much like to have. It has four legs with hooves on the end of them, and a mane and a tail, and you can ride on it, and it's got four letters beginning with P and ending in Y. Can you guess?"

Puddle gave a yap.

"I thought you would," Sophie said. "I just wish I could have one of my own, but I don't suppose I'll ever be that lucky."

Just then Tomboy stood up and stretched herself, and then padded across the lawn – from right to left – in front of the garden seat.

"Yikes!" said Sophie softly to Puddle. "A black

cat coming from the right-hand side is always lucky, Aunt Al told me that, ages ago."

When she had put Beano back in his hutch, Sophie plodded off to find her mother.

"Mummy," she said. "I'm a good rider, aren't I? Meg Morris said so."

Meg Morris was the owner of Cloverlea Stables, and also of Dolly, Tomboy's only daughter.

"Yes, Sophie," her mother said. "You ride very well."

"Well then, d'you think I'll ever have a pony of my own?"

"Before you get to be a lady farmer, d'you mean?"

"Yes. While I'm still young."

"Do you want an honest answer?"

"Yes."

"No."

"Oh."

"To begin with, we've nowhere to put a pony. Second, they're very expensive to buy in any case, and to keep. I'm sorry, Sophie love, but I'm afraid you'll just have to forget the idea."

Sophie nodded.

"I just thought I'd ask," she said.

"Tell you what," her mother said. "It'll be the Easter holidays soon, and then I'll pay for you to have a ride on one of Meg Morris's ponies. Would you like that?"

"Yes, please," said Sophie.

She patted her mother, which meant "Thank you very much", and then she said, "Do they have a riding stables anywhere near where Aunt Al lives?"

"I don't know."

"Perhaps she's got a pony. She did have one

once, called Frisk, but that was in 1920, so I expect
he'll have died."

Sophie's mother smiled.

"They certainly used to keep horses at Balnacraig,"
she said. "I remember seeing the stable block, with
a little white clock tower on top. Daddy and I had
our honeymoon in Scotland, and we went to visit
Aunt Al while we were there. We walked round
the farm."

"What farm?" said Sophie.

"Hers."

"She never told me she was a lady farmer," said
Sophie.

"She isn't," her mother said. "The land belongs
to her but it is let out to a neighbouring farmer.
In the old days, Aunt Al's father used to breed
Highland cattle, I believe."

"I've seen pictures of them! They've got long tously hair," said shaggy Sophie, "and long horns, and they're a lovely goldy colour."

"That's right."

"How big is the farm?" said Sophie.

"I don't really know. Smallish for Scotland, I think."

"How long is it before we go to Scotland?"

"Oh, goodness, it's more than three months away. You'll just have to be patient. Remember the old rhyme,

> *Patience is a Virtue.*
> *Virtue is a Grace.*
> *Grace is a little girl*
> *Who wouldn't wash her face."*

Grace sounded much nicer than Dawn, Sophie thought. Dawn was probably always washing her face.

She rubbed the tip of her nose.

"Mum," she said, "when I'm old enough, d'you think Aunt Al would let the farm to me?"

"Sophie, my love," her mother said, "you're not eight yet, and Aunt Al's going to be eighty-three in the autumn. So if you're talking about when you're twenty, let's say, then Aunt Al would be – let me see – ninety-five!"

"That's OK," said Sophie. "She told me she's going to live to be a hundred."

In Which Sophie Wins a Prize

When the Easter holidays began, Sophie was not slow to remind her mother of her promise. Before breakfast on the very first morning she said, "Will you be ringing up the stables today?"

"The stables?"

"Yes. Cloverlea Stables. *You* know."

"Oh yes, of course," said her mother, and after breakfast she did. Sophie did not listen to her mother talking on the phone. She sat in another room with her fingers crossed, and only when she heard her mother ring off did she go to her and say, "Well?"

"Well," said Sophie's mother, "Meg's a bit busy at the moment, organizing an 'Own-a-Pony Day'."

"What's that?" said Sophie.

"It's a whole day event that she runs – first a grooming competition, then a treasure hunt on foot, then a quiz, then a riding lesson, and then in the afternoon, after a picnic lunch, there's a gymkhana. It would be a lucky child who had all that, wouldn't it?"

"It would," said Sophie.

"Well, you're a lucky child."

"Yikes!" shouted Sophie. "Wicked! Mummy, you're ace!"

When "Own-a-Pony Day" came, Sophie had a marvellous time. There were nine other girls and three boys, and Meg Morris gave them each a number to wear. Sophie was Number Thirteen.

She certainly didn't have any luck in the morning. Some of the other children were quite a bit older, and could reach higher up their ponies when grooming them, and run faster in the treasure hunt on foot, and answer harder questions in the quiz.

But in the afternoon it was different…

Back home afterwards, everyone wanted to know how well Sophie had done.

"Did you win a prize?" asked Mark.

Sophie nodded.

"What for?" asked Matthew.

"Gymkhana," said Sophie.

"Jim Carner?" they said. "Who's he?"

"It's a sort of a sports event on horseback," their mother said.

"What did you win?" asked Sophie's father.

"Oh, just a rosette," said Sophie offhandedly.

"Oh. What colour was it?"

"What does it matter what colour it was?" asked the twins.

"There are different ones, for first, second, third or fourth prize. I can't remember exactly which is which," said Sophie's father. "Tell us, Sophie."

"Green is for fourth place," Sophie said. "Yellow is for third. Blue is for second. And red is for first."

"Well, go on, tell us," everyone said. "What colour was yours?" and Sophie, grinning all over her face, drew from her pocket a red rosette.

*　　*　　*

Sophie's springtime triumph on "Own-a-Pony
Day" was matched, in midsummer, by the twins'
customary successes on the school's Sports Day.
Matthew and Mark were forever racing one
another, and as usual they beat the other boys
in most of the races.

Sophie was not much good at running, though
once, when she was five, she had won the infants'

egg-and-spoon race. This year she didn't win anything (though she tried hard enough), but she didn't mind too much. To have won that red rosette at the gymkhana had been enough. She had fixed it to her bedroom wall with Blu-Tack, underneath the picture of Shorty.

"I'm sorry, my dears," she said to Blossom, April, May and Measles, "but it has to go with a horse, even though it is rather a short horse."

Anyway, Sophie's mind hadn't really been on Sports Day. All she could think about was that in a week's time the summer term would be over at long last, and then they would all be setting off to stay with Aunt Al.

As the day of departure drew near, the children's father got out his motoring atlas to show them where they were going.

"It's a heck of a long way," he said. "It'll take us a couple of days."

"How far is it?" they said.

"About six hundred miles."

"If you went at sixty miles an hour …" said Matthew.

"…we'd be there in ten hours," said Mark.

Sophie watched her father's finger tracing the route on the map, from quite near the bottom of England to quite near the top of Scotland.

"Don't be silly," she said to her brothers. "You can't go up to Scotland at sixty miles an hour. Can't you see – it's uphill, all the way to the top of the Highlands."

"It's not," they said. "It's just going from south to north."

"Exactly," said Sophie. "Going up. After all, you

wouldn't say 'I'm going *down* to the North Pole', would you?"

No amount of explanation would change Sophie's mind about this, and when they did set off on the long drive, she remarked at regular intervals that it would be better on the return journey, as they'd be going downhill all the way.

In fact, when at last the family arrived at Balnacraig, Sophie was fast asleep in her seat belt.

"Wake up, Sophie!" they all said. "We're here."

Sophie opened her eyes to see that they had drawn up on a sweep of gravel before a tall grey house. It had a great many long narrow windows and, above a flight of stone steps, a massive oak front door, which now opened to show a familiar small figure.

Aunt Al came down the steps on her thin bird's

legs to greet them all – the grown-ups with a kiss, the boys with a hug. She came to Sophie last, looking, with her sharp blue eyes and her thin beaky nose, more birdlike than ever, and, knowing Sophie, attempted neither kiss nor hug, but held out her hand, bony and curled like a bird's claw. Sophie took it.

"How de do, Sophie?" said Aunt Al, and, "I'm very well," said Sophie and they grinned at one another.

The children spent the rest of that first day exploring the many tall dark rooms of the old house, right up to the attics that ran the length of it beneath its steep slate roof, decorated with many strange turrets and battlements.

Then there was the stable block, with its clock tower above, and inside, a double row of stabling divided by wooden partitions topped by iron rails.

On some of the doors, names were still dimly visible – MAJOR, STARLIGHT, DUCHESS – and on one, Sophie saw with delight, was written FRISK. There were no horses within now, no stamp of hooves upon the cobbled floor, but the smell was still there, Sophie thought, a faint smell of horse and hay and harness.

Last thing that night, Aunt Al came up to say goodnight, in the little attic bedroom which was to be Sophie's for the holiday, and Sophie said to her, "You never told me you were a lady farmer."

"Well, I'm not, strictly speaking," said Aunt Al. "The land that I own is let out to a neighbouring farmer, Mr Grant."

"How much land?" said Sophie.

"Not a lot. Just over a hundred and fifty acres."

"Yikes!" said Sophie softly. "That's a lot. Can we go and see it tomorrow?"

"If you like."

"Just you and me?"

"I dare say it will be just you and me," said Aunt Al. "I know your mother is looking forward to taking things easy and putting her feet up a bit, and your father will want to go down to the loch."

"Loch Ness?"

"No, no, just a wee lochan, but there are fish to be had and I know he's keen to teach Matthew and Mark how to handle a rod. So you and I will walk down to the farm and see Mr Grant."

And after breakfast next morning they did.

Mr Grant was big and Mrs Grant was small and both of them had the sort of smiling faces that made Sophie like them straight away.

"This is my great-great-niece," Aunt Al said.

"She has a wee bit of a look of you about her, Miss Alice," said Mrs Grant. "Maybe not the features so much, but the expression. A determined person, I'd say."

"You'd be right," said Aunt Al, and to Mr Grant she said, "Is Lucky ready?"

"He is," said Mr Grant, and he went off across the yard.

"Who's Lucky?" said Sophie.

"He belongs to Mr and Mrs Grant's daughter," said Aunt Al, "but she's grown out of him, and they've very kindly agreed to lend him to you while you're here. Look."

And Sophie looked and saw the farmer leading out a stocky brown pony that looked as if it had just come through a hedge backwards.

As a delighted Sophie stood at his head,
patting him and telling him what a fine fellow
he was, there was quite a likeness between them.

"His coat's in a mess, Miss Alice," said Mr Grant.

"He wants grooming badly. But you told me that..."

"I told you," said Aunt Alice, "that if Sophie's going to ride him, then she's going to groom him. OK, Sophie?"

"OK!" said Sophie, and to the farmer she said, "Please, I shall want some warm water and a body-brush and a curry-comb and a dandy brush," and she grabbed Lucky's halter and said, "Walk on!" in so determined a voice that the pony immediately obeyed.

"I was right," said Mrs Grant.

Later that morning, Sophie, wearing a hard hat that had belonged to the Grants' daughter, rode Lucky up the long drive to Balnacraig. Mr Grant had already driven Aunt Al home because she was feeling a bit tired, and she was sitting in a chair on the lawn with Sophie's mother.

"Here comes the horsegirl," she said. "What a nice sturdy little pony," said Sophie's mother. "Apart from the difference in colour, he reminds me of Bumblebee that Sophie rode in Cornwall."

"Lucky suits her well," said Aunt Al. "Perhaps the Grants would sell him to you."

"Oh, Aunt Al!" laughed Sophie's mother. "Wherever would we keep him? Even if we could afford him."

"Ah well," said Aunt Al. "You never know."

In Which Sophie Hears Sad News

Sophie never forgot those ten August days spent at Balnacraig. She had Lucky to ride, with Puddle running beside them, and she had big black Ollie to pet, and the weather was fine, the scenery was beautiful, and on top of all that they were fed like hunters by Aunt Al's housekeeper, Mrs McCosh.

Mrs McCosh had been with Aunt Al's family all her working life.

"She started as a young girl, helping in the kitchen, while my parents were still alive," Aunt Al told Sophie, "and then later she turned out to be a splendid cook. Now she looks after the house, and me too, for I'm not as young as I was. I don't know what I'd do without Eilie McCosh."

"What about Mr McCosh?" Sophie asked. "Is he dead?"

"Well," said Aunt Al, "between you and me and the gatepost, he was never actually alive. You see, Eilie never married, but she likes to be known as 'Mrs' McCosh. It sounds right for a housekeeper, she says."

"She makes yummy cakes," Sophie said. "And she lets me lick out the bowls."

Sophie and the housekeeper had hit it off straight away. To look at, Mrs McCosh was the opposite of Aunt Al. She was large, with a round brown face and strong arms and sturdy legs. If Aunt Al looked like a little bird, Mrs McCosh was more of a big teddy bear.

"I'll tell you something, Sophie," she said one day, "Miss Alice is very fond of your daddy – he's the only member of her family that bothers about her – and of your mother of course, and your brothers, too. But you're her favourite, anyone with half an eye can see that."

Sophie felt very pleased at this. "She's my favourite great-great-aunt," she said.

"How many great-great-aunts have you?"

"Just her. She's going to live to be a hundred, did you know?"

"Is that what Miss Alice told you?"

"Yes."

On the last afternoon of their stay, Sophie asked Aunt Al if she would like to go for a walk and Aunt Al said she would, but not too far.

"You feeling tired then?" asked Sophie.

"A bit."

"It must be tiring having us lot staying."

Aunt Al smiled.

"No, it's not that," she said.

"Can we go as far as the farm?" Sophie asked. "I want to say goodbye to Lucky."

"Of course," said Aunt Al.

At the farm Mr and Mrs Grant came out to say their goodbyes.

"So you're away home tomorrow?" Mrs Grant said to Sophie.

"Yes," said Sophie. "I don't want to go. I shall miss Lucky like anything."

"He'll miss you," said Mr Grant. "He's taken quite a fancy to you."

Sophie stroked Lucky's velvety muzzle.

"I wish you were mine," she said.

"One of these fine days," said Aunt Al, "you might have a pony of your own."

"Miss Alice is right," said Mr Grant. "You might be lucky too."

"Fancy living on that nice farm," said Sophie as they walked home. They reached a rough seat that stood by the side of the drive, and Aunt Al sat down for a moment to rest.

"D'you think you could fancy living there one day, Sophie?" she said.

"I would!" exclaimed Sophie. "But I'd need an awful lot of Farm Money to buy it, wouldn't I?"

"You might," said Aunt Al, "and then again, you might not."

That evening Mrs McCosh produced a splendid supper, which included two fine trout, one caught by Matthew, one by Mark. These were the young anglers' very first catches, and no one was surprised that the fish were of an identical size and weight.

"It's been a wonderful holiday, Aunt Al," Sophie's father said.

"Marvellous," said her mother. "Hasn't it, children?"

"Brill," said the twins with their mouths full.

Sophie didn't say anything.

"Well, Sophie?" said her mother.

"I should like to live here," said Sophie simply.

"I should like it very much if you did," said Aunt Al, "and so, I think, would Mrs McCosh. She tells me you have the makings of a cook."

"But I fear," said Sophie's father, "that tomorrow we must all head home. Perhaps, Aunt Al, you could come and visit us again before long?"

"I shall look forward to that," said Aunt Al.

"It's downhill all the way," said Sophie.

Early next morning they were on their way.

Sophie didn't like goodbyes, and, when her turn came, she was going to stick out her hand as usual. But then suddenly – she didn't know why – she rushed and flung her arms round Aunt Al's skinny middle.

Then they were off, down the long drive of Balnacraig, while behind them two figures, one small and birdlike, one large and bearlike, stood waving farewell, while Ollie rubbed himself against their different-sized legs.

Two days later Tomboy was doing the same thing to Sophie. She seemed pleased to see her back, and Beano, Sophie thought, wiffled his nose more than usual. The next-door neighbour, Sophie considered, had looked after them well.

Matthew and Mark,
fishing forgotten for
now, thought only of
football and their chances of playing for the school
in the coming term. Sophie had no such ambitions
about netball. Small and determined though she
was, she knew that in this game it was an advantage
to be a beanpole, like Dawn. But she was looking
forward to the start of the term, for she would
now be a junior and could, at last, do judo. I don't
suppose Dawn will do it though, she thought. Pity.

Some weeks after the children had gone back to school, the family was sitting in the kitchen having breakfast, when the phone rang. Sophie's father got up and went out of the room to answer it. He was away some time, and when he returned, the three children had gone to get ready for school.

Sophie's mother took one look at her husband's face and said, "What is it?"

"That was Mrs McCosh," said Sophie's father heavily, "ringing from Balnacraig."

"Aunt Al – she's ill? What did Mrs McCosh say?"

"She said, 'I'm sorry to have to tell you that Miss Alice died last night.'"

"Oh, no!"

"It was all very peaceful, apparently. She had told Mrs McCosh she was feeling a bit tired and would go to bed early, and she just died in her sleep. Not a bad way to go."

"We must tell the children."

"Not now. Let's get them off to school, and we'll tell them this evening."

When the time came, Sophie's father didn't beat about the bush. Sophie and the two boys were watching television, and as their programme finished, he switched the TV off and said, "Listen, all of you. I'm afraid there's some sad news. Aunt Al has died."

They stared at him for a moment, and then Matthew said, "When did she die?"

"Last night."

"What did she die of?" asked Mark.

"Old age, I suppose we must say. She was nearly eighty-three, you know."

"But she told me she was going to live to be a hundred," Sophie said.

"I'm afraid she was wrong, Sophie love," said her mother. "She died very peacefully, Mrs McCosh said, just slipped away in her sleep. You must try not to be too sad, she wouldn't have wanted you to be."

For a little while the children said nothing, Matthew and Mark because they couldn't think what to say, and Sophie because she had a big lump in her throat. After a minute she said gruffly, "What about Ollie?"

"Oh, I'm sure Mrs McCosh will look after Ollie," her father said.

Sophie nodded. Then she got up and went out of the room.

Looking through the window, they saw her

plodding
down the
path to the
potting-shed.

Inside it,
Sophie stood
looking
at the big
white rabbit
that had been
a gift from her great-great aunt.

She remembered the day when she and
Aunt Al had walked down to the potting-shed
together, and Aunt Al had said, "Shut your eyes,
Sophie," and she'd said, "Why?" and Aunt Al had
said, "Surprise." and then, once they were inside,
"You can look now."

And when she had opened her eyes, there was Beano!

Now, as she looked at him, her eyes filled.

Then she sniffed loudly, twice.

Then, even though she had never approved of crying, Sophie burst out into a really good howl.

In Which Sophie Says Goodbye

The following week Sophie's father drove up to Scotland once again, this time for his great-aunt's funeral. To take the children out of school for another twelve-hundred-mile round trip was not, they decided, a good idea, so Sophie's mother stayed behind to look after them all.

"What's more," he said, "I have to come back

307

via London. Aunt Al's solicitors want to see me, about her will."

When at last he reached home again – quite late one evening, the children were all fast asleep – Sophie's mother said, "You must be worn out. How did it all go?"

"The funeral, you mean? I was surprised, the little church was full. Lots of local people, and Mrs McCosh of course, and Mr Grant the farmer and his wife. Aunt Al was very well liked, it's plain."

"No one from the family?"

"Only me."

"And you went to see the solicitors?"

"Yes, I did. You had better sit down."

"Why?"

"Apart from a bequest to Mrs McCosh, Aunt Al has left her entire estate to us."

Sophie's mother
did sit down –
with a bump.

"Balnacraig,
you mean?"

"Everything,"
said Sophie's
father. "The house
and grounds,
the contents of
the house, the farm,
and all her money – which
is a great deal. My great-aunt was, it seems, a very
rich old lady. She changed her will quite recently,
the solicitor told me, and she has made a special
provision for our children, too. There's a large
sum of money in trust for Matthew and an exactly

similar amount, you'll not be surprised to hear, for Mark. They'll have the use of it at eighteen."

"And Sophie?"

"No money for Sophie. Something that will please her much more."

"What?"

"The farm at Balnacraig. Mr Grant is to continue as tenant until Sophie reaches the age of eighteen, and then, if she still wishes, she will realize her ambition."

"To be a lady farmer!"

"If she's changed her mind by then, well, it will be hers to sell."

"She won't change her mind!"

"There is something that I haven't told you though," said Sophie's father to his wife. "All this – the property, the money, the children's share in it, everything – depends upon one condition: that we do not sell Aunt Al's house, but move to Scotland and live in Balnacraig ourselves."

"Oh!" said Sophie's mother. "That would be wonderful. But…"

"But what?"

"Our friends here – the children's school – your job."

"We shall make other friends, and Scottish schools are very good, and it's quite possible my firm might have a job for me up there. If not, I'll find another. Anyway, we shan't starve!"

Next day they said to the children, "We're thinking of moving."

"Where to?" said Mark.

"Scotland."

"Where in Scotland?" said Matthew.

"To the Highlands."

"Where in the Highlands?" said Sophie.

"Balnacraig. Aunt Al has left the house to us in her will. It's ours now!"

Matthew and Mark positively gabbled with excitement. Could they have their own fishing-rods, could they learn to ski, could they go mountaineering, could they go to Hampden Park to see the soccer internationals, how soon could they move?

Somehow or other – afterwards they never knew how they managed it – Sophie's father and mother did all the things that had to be done, to be ready for the move at the end of the autumn term.

By now, they had told the boys that Aunt Al

had left them each a sum of money for when
they were grown up.

"Wow!" they said.

"How much?" said Matthew.

"A lot."

"A hundred pounds?" said Mark.

"A bit more than that."

"What about Sophie?" they said.

"Oh, she's been left something, too."

Later, her parents asked Sophie whether she
fancied the idea of going to live at Balnacraig.

"I told you before," said Sophie. "I should like to
live there. Very much. But I'm not coming unless
Tomboy and Beano and Puddle come too."

"Of course they will."

"Will Mrs McCosh still be there?"

"We'll have to see. She may want to retire."

"She can't take Ollie," said Sophie. "He is Tomboy's son, remember, and I bred him and I gave him to Aunt Al and I'm sure she would want me to have him now. So will Ollie be mine?"

"If you like."

"And shall I be able to ride Lucky?"

"I'm sure Mr Grant will let you."

"OK," said Sophie. "I'll come."

At last everything was settled. They had found a buyer for their house, they made all the arrangements for the removal of everything they were taking with them, they settled upon a new school for the children, not far from Balnacraig.

"It'll feel funny to be leaving your friends," Sophie's mother said to her, "but you'll soon make other ones. Still, I expect you'll miss some of the children, won't you?"

"Not Dawn," said Sophie.

"Nor Duncan," she added.

"But what about Andrew? I thought you were engaged to him."

"He could always come to stay," said Sophie.

"It's rather a long way to come. He might not want to."

"He will. I'll tell him, when I go to tea with him tomorrow."

"On the last day of term? Has Andrew's mother invited you?"

"No, but she will. I'll tell him to tell her to."

And she did.

And he did.

At the farm, Andrew's father and mother asked Sophie all about Balnacraig, but after tea Andrew seemed more interested in watching sport on telly. He did not seem too bothered that his fiancée was about to go and live six hundred miles away, and only made his usual reply to her remarks.

"Next year," Sophie said to him, "you can come and stay in Scotland."

"Oh, all right."

"And mind you keep on saving up your pocket money."

"What for?"

"So that we'll have a nice home when we get married, of course."

"Oh, all right."

When Sophie's mother arrived to collect her, Andrew was still glued to the television set.

"Andrew!" his mother said. "Sophie's going. Aren't you coming to say goodbye?"

At the front door, the engaged couple stood
facing one another.

"You'll miss Sophie, won't you, Andrew?" his
mother said.

Andrew nodded.

"Goodbye," he said.

It was plain he was anxious to get back to his programme.

"Now don't forget what I told you," said Sophie.

"What about?"

"About the money. Saving. *You* know."

"Oh, all right."

"The trouble with Andrew," said Sophie to her mother as they made their way home, "is that he doesn't consecrate."

"Concentrate, you mean."

"I mean, he doesn't listen to what I say."

"Perhaps you'd better not marry him then."

"I shan't," said Sophie, "unless he gets his father's farm when he's grown up."

"But just suppose," said her mother, "that when

you're grown up, you should have a farm of your own?"

"Oh, well then," said Sophie, "I shouldn't need to marry Andrew. Because I'd be a lady farmer, wouldn't I?"

"You will," her mother said. "The boys probably never told you, but Aunt Al left them a lot of money."

But not me, thought Sophie. Funny, she knew I needed more Farm Money.

"She left you something, too, for when you're grown up."

"What?" said Sophie.

"The farm at Balnacraig."

In Which Sophie's Lucky

O n Christmas Day – Sophie's eighth birthday –
the three children were only given quite
small presents. They didn't mind, because they'd
been told that when, in a week's time, they'd made
the move to Scotland, there would be a very special
present waiting for each of them at the other end.

"And don't think you'll get such presents every
year," their father told them. "These are to
celebrate our coming to Balnacraig to live."

* * *

When at last they all arrived at their new home,
it was very late and everyone was dog-tired
(including Puddle). Mrs McCosh, who had said she
would stay on as long as they wanted her,

had supper ready, and afterwards the children
went to bed. No amount of pleading would
persuade their parents to show them those three
special presents that night.

"First thing after breakfast tomorrow," their
father said. "I promise."

Sophie lay in bed in her new room, the little attic
bedroom where she had slept when Aunt Al was
still alive, and looked at her pictures, newly hung
upon the walls, of Blossom, and April and May,
and Measles, and Shorty.

Tired as she was, her last thoughts before sleep
were of her animals. Puddle was in his bed in the
kitchen. Beano was in his hutch in a loose-box, a
warmer and drier place than the old potting-shed.
As for Tomboy, Sophie knew that Ollie was busy
showing his mother round the place.

All was well.

First thing after breakfast next morning, Sophie's father said, "Right. Time now for your rather late Christmas presents, and Sophie, yours will be Christmas and birthday combined."

"Where are they?" the children asked.

"In the stable block," their mother said, "but no rushing ahead, mind. We'll all go down together."

So they did, and there, just inside the main door of the stables, were two brand-new mountain bikes, one red, one blue.

"The red one's for you, Matthew," said his father.

"And," said his mother, "the blue one's for you, Mark."

"Oh, thanks! Thanks a million!" they shouted, and each grabbed hold of his bike and dashed off.

Sophie looked around, but she couldn't see

any sign of a present for herself. Just then she heard a sudden sharp noise, at the far end of the row of stalls. If she hadn't known that there were no horses now at Balnacraig (except for Lucky down at the farm), she could have sworn it was the sound of a hoof stamping upon the cobbled floor.

She looked at her parents. They were smiling.

"Your present is a specially big one," they said.

"For Christmas and for your eighth birthday."

"Have a look down at the far end."

Sophie plodded down the stables till she came to the end stall of the row, the one with the name FRISK above it.

There stood Lucky.

"What's Lucky doing up here?" said Sophie.

"Why isn't he down at the farm?"

"Because he doesn't live there any more," her
mother said.

"Because we bought him from the Grants," said
her father.

Sophie gulped.

"For me?" she said.

"For you," they said. "For your very own."

For once Sophie didn't shout, "Yikes!"

For once she wasn't able to speak at all.

At last she managed to mutter in a rather
strangled voice, "Thanks, Mummy. Thanks, Dad,"
and she patted them both. Then she went to pat
Lucky.

"Hello again, my dear," she said, and she put
an arm round his neck and gave him a hug, and
looked up at her father and mother and grinned
all over her face.

"Happy?" they said.

"I'm the happiest," said Sophie, "that I've ever been in the whole of my life."

THE END

Dick King-Smith (1922–2011), a former dairy farmer, is one of the world's favourite children's book authors. He won the Guardian Fiction Prize for *The Sheep-Pig* (later filmed as *Babe*), was named Children's Book Author of the Year in 1991 and won the 1995 Children's Book Award for *Harriet's Hare*.

His titles for Walker include the Sophie books, *Aristotle*, *Lady Lollipop* and its sequel, *Clever Lollipop*.

David Parkins has illustrated a number of children's books, including the picture books *Prowlpuss* (shortlisted for the 1994 Kurt Maschler Award, and the 1995 Smarties Book Prize) and *Webster J. Duck*, written by Hans Christian Andersen Award-winner Martin Waddell. David was born in Brighton but now lives in Canada.

Sophie's fond of most creatures
– especially little ones like snails –
but there's one she cannot stand:
her prissy new neighbour, Dawn!

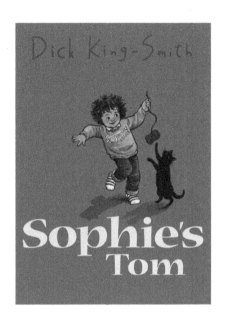

On her fifth birthday Sophie gets
a model farm and lots of toy animals.
What she wants most of all, though, is a
real animal – a cat like Tom, for example…

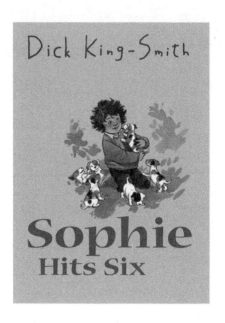

Dick King-Smith

Sophie
Hits Six

Sophie gets some new animals
– including four new kittens –
finds a farming friend
and enters the sporting arena!

Dick King-Smith

LADY
LOLLIPOP

illustrated by Jill Barton

"I wanna pig!" yells right royal brat Princess Penelope.

And she gets one. But Lollipop is no ordinary pig.

When people look into her bright, intelligent eyes,

it seems to change them. For the better…

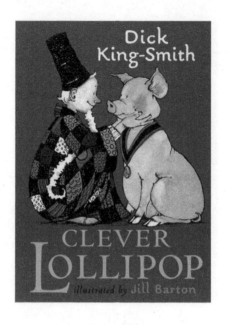

The King and Queen engage a Royal tutor for
Princess Penelope. But Collie Cob, the Conjuror,
is no ordinary teacher. Whether you're a person or a pig
he can teach you almost anything. As if by magic…